The Hunted Tribe
Book 2: Rocket's Red Glare

By Roma Gray

Cover Art by Kendall R. Hart

©2019 Roma Gray

ALL RIGHTS RESERVED.

This book contains material protected under International and Federal Copyright Laws and Treaties. Any unauthorized reprint or use of this material is prohibited. No part of this book, including the cover and photos, may be reproduced or transmitted in any form or by any means, electronic or mechanical, including photocopying, recording, or by any information storage and retrieval system without express written permission from the author / publisher. All rights reserved.

Any resemblance to persons, places living or dead is purely coincidental.

This is a work of fiction.

This is a Roma Gray Trick-or-Treat Thriller

This book is age appropriate for the young, the old, and everyone in between.

Enjoy!

Chapter 1

Terror gripped Sean's mind and heart, squeezing tighter and tighter like a metal vice.

He stood in his dark bedroom with his hand on the doorknob, frozen in fear. A glance at his clock told him it was nearly four a.m. He had to go downstairs now before he chickened out, he had to.

But what if...?

Sean quickly pushed this thought from his mind, turned the door handle and exited the room.

You've got to do this, Sean!

Creeping to his grandmother's bedroom, he silently opened the door and peeked inside. In the shadows, he could see the outline of her figure lying in bed, breathing in and out in the peaceful rhythm of sleep. He released a sigh of relief, gently closed the door and continued down the hall.

Creak...

Sean paused, his heart racing in his chest. He hadn't made the sound nor had his grandmother—the sound came from downstairs.

His head became light and fuzzy, while his knees threatened to buckle. For the briefest moment he hesitated, wanting to turn around and run back to his bedroom, close the door and hide under his covers.

No! screamed his mind. *This is the third night in a row that you've chickened out. This time you're going to do it. There's nothing down there—not really.*

It was the 'not really' part that, in fact, terrified him. But, at the same time, he knew he couldn't continue to

live this way. He had to face this...
Just get it done!

Although no one could see him, Sean nodded in reply. Steeling himself to his mission, he stood up straight, squared his shoulders, and walked down the stairs with a renewed determination in his gait.

It was even darker downstairs, but he didn't dare turn on a light. The blackness surrounding him rapidly dissolved away his false bravado, and fear once again flooded back in. With trembling hands outstretched in front of him, Sean moved through the living room. After several near falls and painful encounters with the furniture, he made it to the study door and slowly opened it. The hinges gave a slight creak, and he cringed as he continued to apply pressure. His destination was just beyond the door; he was almost there now.

Sean spent several days searching the internet, trying to find anything on the man who died, Gregg Redcrow. He had managed to score quite a bit of information. The man, indeed, was a Native American (he had claimed to be Sioux, or was Sioux, depending on your point of view) and taught college classes on dinosaurs. But the reports stated he was a victim of a road rage incident, not an animal attack. His throat had been slit after a confrontation with another driver who had apparently rammed Gregg's wife's truck into a ditch, killing her as well. Unfortunately, the reports also said there were no witnesses or arrests.

He remembered the night that Gregg had died—it was the night his grandmother disappeared. Sean had been sick and gone into her bedroom room around midnight, hoping she could recommend something to help him feel better. Instead, all he found was an empty, unslept-in bed. He didn't see her again until late afternoon the next day. She gave the excuse that she couldn't sleep, so she went for a walk, then took the morning ferry to the mainland to go shopping.

But, is that what really happened?

Grandma had the time to get there and back, no doubt about it. She could have done it. She could have killed Gregg and his wife...

For a moment, he shuddered at the thought.

Am I really considering this? Do I really believe my grandmother—the woman who took care of me when I was sick, the woman who made me cookies and listened to me when I had problems, the one and only person in the entire universe who has always stood by me—is actually a psychotic murderer?

But how could he think otherwise? Dr. Ann Wedge, his grandmother's former psychiatrist, traveled all the way to Elk Island to warn him that she was afraid his grandmother was going to harm Gregg. She said that his grandmother was so obsessed with this invented monster of hers, the Grishla, she might actually try to make it look like the creature attacked him to support her claims of its existence.

The Grishla. Sean rolled his eyes at the thought. His grandmother had been quite crafty, sucking him into her fantasy. She had told him that he wasn't even part Cherokee, that all of them—his grandmother, dad, Gregg and himself—were actually descendants of a fictitious Native American tribe called the Dwanake. They were all being hunted by this Grishla, a dinosaur animal spirit. The craziest part of the whole story was she said that Sean was a powerful witch who was destined to save his tribe from this terrible monster.

It was lunacy, pure lunacy! He still couldn't believe how easily he fell for it. Of course, in his own defense, she had played her hand well.

First, she used the monster from his own nightmare to scare him. As Ann told him, this dream was probably a result of his grandmother telling him stories about the Grishla when he was a young child. Too young to recall the stories, but old enough that his subconscious still remembered. After that, well, the rest was history. Sean had the nightmare, must have mentioned it to his mom, who then probably told his grandmother and *that's* what gave her the idea to invite him out to the island for the summer so she could spend 24-7 brainwashing him!

The cleverest part was how she convinced him he had magical powers. She gave him a feather in a glass box and told him that he could levitate the feather through telepathy. Ann explained to him this was an old, well-documented magicians' trick from the 1800's: The feather in the box was actually controlled by a person breathing near it, disrupting air currents feeding into holes in the seams of the box, causing the feather to move. The second oldest magicians' trick was a simple pad of paper that his grandmother gave him, telling him he could close his eyes and magic would guide his hand, telling him unseen truths. She said this was called 'automatic writing' or 'free association' and therapists used this technique to aid the patient's subconscious mind in communicating with them. Well, that sure worked well. The resulting message said simply, 'There is no such thing as magic, and the legend of the Grishla is a lie.' His subconscious knew the truth, even if he didn't.

I'm such an idiot, he thought to himself.

Returning to the present, Sean quietly closed the study door. Trying not to let the tell-tale creak of the hinges rattle his nerves, he turned on the light and headed to his grandmother's old desk.

He quickly opened the drop-down flap on the front of the desk, hoping he would find what he was looking for—or perhaps hoping he wouldn't. Unfortunately, find it he did. On top of all the papers was a note that had the name 'Gregg Redcrow' scrawled across the top. Stapled to the note was the man's information: phone number, address, and map to his house.

Oh no.... Sean felt his heart drop into his stomach like a rock plunging into an icy lake. *She knew where he lived...she could have done it...she really could have done it!*

At that moment, he heard another creak—this time coming from the floorboards directly behind him.

Sean gasped, whirled around, and there, standing just a few feet away, was another teenager. The teen wore the same red t-shirt and blue jeans, had the same long, black bangs hanging down over his high cheekbones and had the same dark brown eyes as Sean; the boy, was in fact, Sean's exact double.

The double stared back at Sean with a mischievous smile.

"Hugo!" gasped Sean.

"Did you miss me?" Hugo snidely remarked. "I'm surprised you finally found the courage to come down here and look through your grandmother's desk. After all, you're such a sniveling little coward. Surely, it wasn't me you were afraid of?"

"You're not real, I invented you," Sean firmly stated, trying to sound brave, yet betraying his fear by backing up into the desk. The sharp corner struck his leg hard, and he involuntarily flinched from the pain. "I invented you. I called you 'Hugo the Jerk.' You're just a label—the name I gave to the negative voices in my head, nothing more!"

Hissing a mocking laugh, Hugo stepped towards him.

"It was your way of separating yourself from your darker side—*from me!*—you little bastard," answered Hugo, a touch of venom in his voice. "You were pretending those negative thoughts didn't come from you, that they came from someone else. Bad things happen when you disown a part of yourself, Sean. Awful, unthinkable things..."

Sean shook his head hard. "No, no, you're not real! You can't do anything to me!"

"What do you say we test that theory?" said Hugo, confidently closing the distance between the two.

Holding his ground, Sean waited for the illusion to stop. Hugo couldn't hurt him, couldn't touch him, the sane part of his mind knew that. He just needed to hold onto that thought, hold on to that one shred of reality.

Then the unthinkable happened.

Hugo's left hand roughly grabbed Sean by the collar, his grip powerful and unyielding. Sean gasped and choked. *No, no! This can't be happening, it can't!* Terror then took full hold as Hugo effortlessly lifted him off the ground. Out of the corner of his eye, Sean caught a flash of gleaming metal in Hugo's right hand. With a maniacal snicker, Hugo slowly raised a sharp blade up to Sean's face.

"Tell me which frightens you more," growled Hugo, a murderous glint in his eyes. "That I'm real or that you are going insane, just like your grandmother?"

Chapter 2

At first, Sean couldn't look away from the gleaming metal blade, but then his gaze abruptly shifted to Hugo's face and their eyes locked.

"You're not Hugo..," growled Sean, his fury erasing the fear.

Hugo's expression changed to one of surprise, and he laughed. "Oh really? Then who am I? Your grandma?"

"You're the Grishla!" Sean stated firmly. "It all makes sense now. You forced Ann to lie to me, tell me she was a doctor at some mental institution and that my grandmother was insane!"

"I don't exactly look like a velociraptor…"

"A Deinonychus," corrected Sean. "But it doesn't matter what your real form is. My grandmother said Gregg owned something called 'The Revealing Stone,' a rock that the witches of the Dwanake tribe, the Trebors, endowed with a powerful spell to force an animal spirit disguised as a human to reveal themselves. It's what got him killed, I'm certain of it, but it tells me something else too. You *are* the Grishla, and you've taken on a human's form¾my form! ¾trying to convince me you're Hugo and that I'm insane!"

Hugo's smile grew broader. "Oh, and I thought that your magic sent me away off the island? I mean, you are supposed to be the great Ultra Witch, destined to

11

save your people from the evil dinosaur animal spirit that hunted your tribe. Now, how could a dumb animal spirit like myself possibly stand a chance against you? But that doesn't matter now does, it? *I am* the Grishla, you've figured me out, and now I will have to kill you!"

Sean's mind raced. *I need a weapon or something... a spell! But what spell? Stop panicking and think! Damn it, think!*

Hugo pulled the blade away from Sean's face—a pair of scissors, he now realized—and pushed it back in his pocket. Then, to his utter surprise, Hugo began to jam his index finger into Sean's temple over and over again.

"Stupid! Stupid! Stupid! Stupid!" he repeated with each jab of his finger.

"Stop that!" came another voice. Someone walked up from behind Hugo, another duplicate of Sean. It was Richard the Sensible, another fictitious alter ego that Sean had invented, his imaginary angel on his shoulder.

Hugo rolled his eyes. "Back off, Richard the Senseless. I'm teaching our young boy here a lesson."

Richard grabbed Hugo's arm and gave him a rough jerk back. Clearly not anticipating a physical attack (albeit a mild one) from his goody-two-shoes counterpart, Hugo abruptly dropped Sean, who landed on his feet with a loud thud.

Richard gasped, turned pale, and looked around. "What's wrong with you two? If we wake up his grandmother..."

"So?" groaned Hugo. "If Sean's best buddy Jimmy didn't notice us when we were harassing Sean at the pit the other day when the two of them decided to work on it on their own, then his grandmother isn't going to see us either."

Richard sighed and replied in a soft voice. "We don't want her catching Sean, either. He has work to

The Hunted Tribe: Rocket's Red Glare

do."

"Work?" asked Sean, startled by how the situation had changed. He didn't know what to think now.

Richard turned to him and placed a gentle hand on his shoulder. "Yes, work. But let's clear up a few things first. Hugo and I can't be the Grishla because there are two of us, right? Even the Grishla can't split himself in two, can he?"

Sean felt a tinge of disappointment as he slowly shook his head. He actually wanted to believe the Grishla was real. Because if it was, his grandmother wasn't crazy¾and neither was he.

Genetics is such a wonderful thing, thought Sean to himself.

"Besides," continued Richard, "think about the other evidence. Jimmy was the only one who got a good look at the creature that attacked you and your friends the night of the camping trip. Later, you told him you knew he was lying and convinced him you wouldn't tell the others. He recanted his story about it being a bear and said it was what again, Sean?"

Sean crossed his arms across his chest and sighed. He then grumbled, "Bigfoot. He said we were being chased by Bigfoot."

Hugo immediately began to snicker. "Bigfoot¾who occasionally ran on all fours while he was chasing you. What kind of an idiot mistakes a bear for Bigfoot? Your best friend is quite the Einstein there, Sean."

Hugo had crossed the line, and Sean charged toward him, fists squeezed into tight balls. Richard quickly grabbed him and pulled him back before he could begin his assault.

"You say whatever you want about me, but don't you dare talk about my friends!" snapped Sean as Richard continued to hold him back.

"Shhh, let it go," pleaded Richard, still struggling with Sean. "Your grandmother is going to hear!"

Sean stopped, and Hugo winked back at him roguishly and threw him a mocking kiss.

"Listen, please, we don't have much time," whispered Richard.

Sean nodded, taking in deep breaths, trying to calm himself. "Fine. What do you want me to do?"

"Well, Hugo and I have been talking about this situation," said Richard, and Sean could feel his eyes growing large. Seeing and feeling his imaginary alter egos in person was bad enough, but to learn they had been talking about him behind his back was even more disturbing. Still, he said nothing as Richard continued. "We decided the only reason you're still seeing us is either: One, you really are going insane like your grandmother..." Sean briefly choked. Even though Richard was supposed to be his nice alter ego, he had a way of blurting out unpleasant truths, never considering the consequence. "Or two, she's still drugging you with those hallucinogenic herbs to boost your 'magical powers' like she did the night of the campfire. Remember? That night you had visions of the Grishla through the eyes of its victims. It was extremely convincing, as I recall."

"What? How could you possibly think she could be doing that still? Are you insa..," Sean stopped abruptly, unable to finish the word. Accusing his imaginary alter-ego of being insane was just too much. "Listen, I found the bottle she was drugging me with, that little pink glass jar that she had out on the counter. It's gone. I threw it into the trash."

"Then why is it I found it hidden in behind her other spices yesterday afternoon?" asked Hugo smugly.

Richard sighed and shook his head. "Sean actually found it, Hugo. He just thought he was you when he did it. Please don't confuse him. The poor boy is frightened enough."

Hugo groaned. "Fine. You found it, Sean. Whatever. Clearly, your grandmother must have noticed it missing and went looking for it in the trash, probably guessing what you did. Now it's back. And it was hidden, which proves she knows it was you."

Richard nodded. "Then you went to the grocery store, picked up some herbs that looked like the hallucinogenic ones, with the plan of replacing them. Right now, this morning, you must do it. Before she uses any more of her weird drugs in your food."

"Of course, you forgot all of this, didn't you?" sneered Hugo. He then pulled out the scissors from his jacket pocket. "Come on, let's get to it before psycho granny wakes up."

Hugo turned and quickly walked out of the study door with Sean and Richard close behind. As they made their way through the living room, Sean watched the other two boys¾his hallucinations¾with fascination. They seemed so real. They cast the same long, sinewy shadows across the darkened living room as he did, and he noticed Hugo's hair was sticking up at an odd angle in the back. *Such detail... So this is what happens when people with high IQ's go nuts, huh?*

At one point, Richard bumped into an end table and yelped, the noise sounding a hundred times louder in the deathly silent house. Sean saw Richard rub his leg where the corner of the table had struck him, and Sean rubbed his own leg in the same spot, noticing his leg did not hurt at all.

So, did I bump into the table and not feel it, or did no one bump into the table and I imagined the whole thing?

The scenario was enough to drive a person out of their mind. Except, of course, he clearly already was out of his mind.

Finally, the three entered the kitchen, and Sean sighed in frustration. Sure enough, there was the little pink glass bottle on the kitchen counter. Again.

Crafty old woman. And determined. She really

believes those herbs will boost my magical powers. Once again, he wondered where she got them. No doubt, some tribe once used them in a religious ceremony for that very purpose, to increase someone's magical powers—which tribe he'd probably never know.

Richard immediately grabbed the bottle, opened the back door, dumped the contents of the pink glass jar outside, quickly moved to the sink, and began washing it out. In the meantime, Hugo pulled out a plastic envelope from his jacket with a label that said 'Italian Herbs', cut open the bag with the pair of scissors he had threatened Sean with earlier, and silently waited as he watched Richard dry the glass bottle.

Sean felt a wave of nausea again. He thought back to his first day on the island and the cookies his grandmother made for his birthday. Since that day, he had felt sick, just like when he was a kid and had cancer. He'd never forget the agony of the chemotherapy he endured back then. This drug-induced illness felt a lot like the chemo.

That should have been a big tip off that you were being drugged, Sean. I guess I should be thankful it wasn't the cancer coming back like I thought.

Sean rubbed his temples as a headache began to form. "If you two are doing everything, why do you need me here?" He asked, suddenly feeling exhausted. He really just wanted to go back to bed.

Richard and Hugo both abruptly stopped what they were doing and turned to look at Sean, shock etched on their features.

"Because we're not really here, Nimrod," chided Hugo.

"We only exist in your head, Sean, remember?" reminded Richard. "You're actually the one doing this."

"Oh...yeah...of course," said Sean, feeling his face flush. "Well...um...carry on then I guess..."

This is one heck of a trip! he thought to himself.

"If it makes you feel any better," said Richard, carefully pouring the herbs into the bottle. "You're probably a little more out of it than usual because you've been inhaling the herbs while you were working to get rid of them. I'm sure you'll feel better soon."

"Uh-huh," replied Sean, doubting he could ever feel better again unless he was lucky enough to forget this entire experience.

Richard and Hugo finished the job and placed the pink glass bottle back to where Hugo—or rather Sean in a drug-induced state—had found them hidden the previous day.

"There, all better now," said Richard with a broad smile. "Hugo and I are leaving now. Go to bed and get some rest."

"And don't forget to call Jimmy," said Hugo pointing to the slip of paper in Sean's hand with Gregg Redcrow's address written on it. "You'll need him to drive you to Gregg's house, assuming you're still determined to investigate his murder. Jimmy's the only one who has access to a car. Besides, he's also the only one of your friends who will take you there no questions asked. You can tell your grandmother you're staying over at his house to go fishing with him after the July 4th get-together with the guys," Hugo then laughed and added, "which is exactly what you're doing¾fishing for clues!"

Sean nodded. He had already worked this part out in his mind. His grandmother told him he needed to focus on his magic lessons the next week, and he knew this would be his last chance to take off for a day without raising any suspicions. He had tried to figure out a way to do this on his own, but without a car, he had no choice but to pull in Jimmy.

Richard and Hugo walked to the kitchen door and opened it. Richard left first, disappearing into the night, but Hugo paused and turned to face Sean.

"Hope you find everything you're looking for."

"Really?" asked Sean, incredulous.

Hugo shrugged. "Sure, why not? I just hope you don't discover that you're the murderer."

Sean let out a short laugh. "I didn't even know the guy!"

"You knew about him," said Hugo. "Your grandmother told you about Gregg in that phone conversation you had with her before you came to the island."

"What? I didn't talk to her on the phone before I came to the island!"

"Yes you did," insisted Hugo. "You also knew where Gregg lived, the same way you knew exactly where that paperwork would be. You found her map and notes the first day you came to the island when you were snooping around."

Sean grunted back, finally getting up to speed. "Nice try. But without a motive…"

"You were being drugged the second you walked into the house," answered Hugo. "You probably can't remember half of what you did those first few days."

Swallowing hard, Sean began to shake his head, "No…no…that's…no…"

A malicious smile crossed Hugo's face, and then he turned around and left, closing the door behind him.

Sean stared at the closed door.

Was Hugo just yanking my chain? Or is true and I just can't remember? And if it is true, does that mean I really am losing my mind and it's not the hallucinogenic herbs? He glanced up at the ceiling and an icy pang of dread slammed into his chest. *If my grandmother is crazy…I could be crazy myself. I could…*

Finally, he shook his head and groaned. The whole idea was absurd—the idea he might have done it and the idea he was listening to a drug-induced hallucination.

"Thank god Ann isn't here to see me," said Sean to himself. "The last thing I need is a doctor from a mental institution seeing me like this. She'd probably have me committed on the spot."

***

Ann lay flat on her back on the small twin bed, still dressed in her blue business suit that she wore the day she met Sean, except now it looked crumpled and disheveled. She stared up at the ceiling with unblinking eyes. Time passed unnoticed by her, as did everything else in the room. A fly landed on her forehead, yet she did not react to the unwanted visitor.

The fly leisurely walked across her forehead, down her nose, and stopped just at her eyelashes. The insect hesitated, washing its face with its front legs, waiting to see if the woman would shoo him away. Seconds passed and the fly finally decided it was safe. Slowly, the fly stepped up and over her eyelashes, walking directly onto the sticky whites of her eyes. Another pause. Still no movement. Feeling bolder, the fly carefully laid a few of its eggs in the inner corner of her eye.

Satisfied with its accomplishment, the fly moved out of her eye, down her face and toward the open gash across her throat where a swarm of fat flies feasted on the edges of the open wound, and large, undulating maggots squirmed in the center.

Chapter Three

"Careful! The steps are pretty shallow," Tom called out to the others climbing the stairs behind him.

"No joke," grumbled Bear. "They're barely big enough for a child's foot! How does your dad get up here?"

"Very carefully," answered Tom, as he pushed open the ceiling hatch.

Bear, Jimmy, and Sean blinked as the harsh light from the hatch suddenly invaded the dark stairwell. Far above them in the distant sky, swirling reds, oranges, and pinks announced the approaching sunset.

As Sean emerged onto the roof of the floating home, he scanned the area. They were surrounded by blue water and a small handful of other floating homes. Tom waved good-naturedly at his neighbors who were all sitting in chairs on their roofs, and they all happily waved back.

With Tom's perfect smile, trim build, designer 'Rocket's Red Glare' brand denim jacket with the American flag on the sleeves, and wavy blonde hair, he once again reminded Sean of an actor or a male model. For a moment, Sean recalled when they first met, he felt intimidated by Tom. Now he realized this said more about his own lack of self-confidence than about Tom. Until this summer, Sean had been a career couch potato with the physique of a pillow to show for it. But, thanks to his improved diet and extensive exercise digging at the pit they found in the forest a few weeks back, Sean was beginning to get into better shape. Lately, he had been sporting his own (albeit slight) muscle tone and a slimmer frame.

He pushed his jaw-length black hair out of his eyes, stood tall and smiled. *You've come a long way, baby!*

"This is a really nice set up," said Bear, straightening his camouflage shirt over his ample build. He was also looking more muscular and trim these days, although his mid-section still hung over his belt a couple inches. Nonetheless, it didn't slow him down with the ladies. Just the other day, Sean noticed at the grocery store yet another cute girl shamelessly flirting with Bear. He wondered if it was his tall height, rugged mountain man appearance, or his perpetual two-day stubble that attracted them. On considering this further, Sean realized what attracted the ladies was probably the entire package that made Bear look like a full grown man in his twenties, rather than a sixteen-year-old boy like the rest of them.

"This is amazing!" announced Jimmy as he lightly bounded up the stairs like a gazelle, with his short, tawny hair and thin, gangly body. Unlike the others, Jimmy hadn't developed any muscle tone over the past few weeks, yet he worked the hardest of the group. He never seemed to change at all. *The guy is an enigma,* thought Sean. "Yep...yep...really amazing!" continued Jimmy.

Tom smiled back at his friends, visibly pleased with the unanimous endorsement. "And the best part is we don't have to worry about animal attacks like what happened on our last outing," he laughed. "Even if an orca gets a few ideas, we're too high up for him or her to reach us."

"So why does your family own both a floating home and a vacation home on the island?" asked Sean.

"This was our first vacation home," said Tom. "Then, when dad made more money, he had the house built. He kept this for mom. She wanted a painting studio."

"Perfect place to see the fireworks," said Bear, dumping the ice from the plastic bag he carried up the stairs into a cooler that was placed between two of the four chairs.

"Yeah, on the few occasions we've returned to the island, I usually try to watch the Fourth of July fireworks display from up here," said Tom, adding the soft drinks he had carried up in his backpack to the cooler. "My mom and dad aren't into it, though; they like to turn in early when they're on vacation."

Sean pulled four paper sacks out of his backpack and placed them on the small table in front of the chairs as the guys settled in. As usual, each one of them brought their own food. Bear and Tom wanted to get take-out, but they all knew Jimmy couldn't afford it. It pained all of them watching him eat his small peanut butter sandwiches, especially since it was so very clear how undernourished Jimmy was. This time, however, Jimmy surprised all of them when he pulled out a huge hoagie sandwich from his lunch bag.

"What's that?" asked Bear, leaning forward to get a better look at Jimmy's lunch. "That's not peanut butter on there, is it?"

"Nope, I'm done with PB sandwiches, at least for a while. Yep, done with them," he said with a smile. "I was looking through a magazine at the store and found a recipe for something called a falafel. They're patties made with seasoned chickpeas and grains. You bread them, then bake them until they're crunchy. Combined with sliced tomatoes, arugula, onion and homemade hot sauce on a bun, they make an incredible sandwich."

"What the hell is arugula?" asked Bear.

"It's like spinach, but it's spicy," said Jimmy. "I grow it in my vegetable garden."

Bear shook his head.

"Why not just buy lunch meat, dude?" asked Bear, beginning to unwrap his own sandwich.

Sean frowned and so did Tom. Bear sometime just didn't get it that Jimmy might be embarrassed about his financial situation.

"Because if I bought lunch meat, it would last me one meal, maybe two, that's why," said Jimmy, matter-of-factly. "I can get a bag of chickpeas and a bag of rye berries for just a few dollars. Plus, I have enough to feed myself and my parents for three days¾with enough left over to make another batch the following week. I'm telling you, these things are a game changer for me, I'll be able to stretch our food budget much farther now. And they taste awesome!"

"Beans and grains?" grumbled Bear. "How good could they taste?"

"They taste as good as you flavor them," said Jimmy. "I made mine hot and spicy."

"I'm with Jimmy on this," said Tom. "My parents and I love to go to this Greek restaurant in Chicago. Man, the falafels are like heaven! They make sandwiches with them there, too. Except they charge about fifteen bucks for theirs."

"Seriously?" asked Jimmy looking at Tom and then back at his sandwich. "My sandwich probably cost about a dollar and some change."

"Even with that big hoagie bun?" asked Sean.

Jimmy laughed. "I make my own bread now, too. The things that cost the most on the sandwich were the tomato and onion. But even that wasn't so bad."

"Aren't you becoming a little too domestic lately?" said Bear. "Home-made hot sauce, home-made fala… fala…uh…bean patties, home-baked bread, home-grown fancy lettuce, and who knows what else? That takes a lot of work."

Jimmy smiled. "Not that much work, and I'm telling you, there's nothing like the taste of homemade food. Especially the fresh baked bread. I'll never go back."

Bear shook his head. "Maybe what you really need to do is get your dad to get off his duff and get a job..."

Tom and Sean simultaneously kicked Bear. He shot them dirty looks, but kept his mouth shut. Jimmy pretended not to notice.

"Let's get settled in, what do you say, guys?" said Tom handing Bear a soda, with a stern look.

Bear took the soda and silently mouthed, *Okay, okay.*

The four sat down in their chairs and began to unwrap their food. Jimmy made exaggerated yummy sounds as he ate his sandwich, a little over-played in Sean's opinion. He knew what his friend was doing: He was trying to convince the guys that he was managing just fine. It was a losing game¾the guys knew the truth; Jimmy's home-life was a disaster.

"Ah, hell! The damn neighbors are at it again, I should have known!" explained Tom suddenly, waving his hand in front of his face, his nose crinkling in disgust as he leaned back and shot a dirty look at the green floating home a short distance away. Sean turned and looked. The family was up on top of their roof, smoke billowing from their grill. *Steaks, I'd wager,* thought Sean. *Damn, that smells good!* But Tom looked less than pleased, and Sean tensed as he awaited his tirade. "Burnt flesh! How completely disgusting! How am I supposed to eat my meal when I have to smell...?"

"Time out! Time out!" said Bear all of a sudden. "Listen up, Capt. Vegan. I get that you're vegan, we all do, but enough already. I'm trying to eat my meal, which I'm sorry, is made with meat. I've had it up to here with you ruining my meals with your gross out descriptions. Just keep it to yourself for once, okay? We're your guests, and I think it's pretty rude of you to say things to turn our stomachs. I want to enjoy my dinner too."

Tom looked slightly shocked. Honestly, Sean was

too. That was an amazingly insightful comment, and quite frankly, he didn't think Bear had it in him.

At first, Tom looked like he was going to get angry, go into one of his speeches again. But then, he seemed to stop himself, considering Bear's word. To Sean's surprise, Tom flushed and said, "I...I hadn't thought of it that way, Bear. I apologize to all of you."

Bear smiled and returned a short nod. Sean also smiled back as did Jimmy.

"No worries, Tom," said Jimmy. "It's all cool here."

"Yep, all cool," said Bear.

Tom looked relieved, as did Sean. *No drama today, guys, please!* thought Sean. *I'm starving, I just want to eat.* Returning his attention to his own sandwich, Sean hastily picked it up and bit into it, and then stopped, shocked by what he tasted. He lifted up the bun to check and confirmed his suspicions.

"I don't believe it," he said. "My grandmother made me a falafel sandwich too..."

"What?" asked Tom, Bear and Jimmy in unison.

"You're making that up," said Bear, finally. "Or you've got falafel on the brain. You never even heard of them before today."

"I do too know what a falafel is; I used to get them at my favorite Indian restaurant in New York. And I'm not making it up."

Sean, opened up his sandwich and held it out to show the others. Jimmy opened his up as well, and then the two boys held the two sandwiches up next to each other for comparison. Not only were they both made with falafels, the patties were made to the same identical size and shape. Both sandwiches also had tomato, onion, and even arugula.

"The bread even looks the same," said Tom, pointing to the hoagie bun.

"Well, my grandmother has always made her own bread," said Sean. "She has dairy and meat allergies and has to be careful."

The Hunted Tribe: Rocket's Red Glare

Sean examined the bread a little closer. Both buns were riddled with wheat and oat bran. They really did look identical. After listening to Jimmy about how much effort went into making his sandwich, it seemed unlikely to the point of being ridiculous that his grandmother would coincidentally make the same identical sandwich on the same exact day.

"That's kind of freaky," said Jimmy. "Yeah, really freaky. Maybe your grandmother is spying on me."

The guys laughed, and Sean forced himself to laugh along, but inside he felt sick. His grandmother had kept him on a Nutritarian diet lately to get him in shape, eliminated not just meat and dairy but processed food as well. Then, all of a sudden, today she surprised him with this special sandwich, even though bread was on his 'can't have' list. That alone seemed out of character, but this duplicate sandwich implied something far more.

Is my grandmother stalking Jimmy? Sean internally shuddered at the thought.

Jimmy had confided in Sean that he found something under his house, a dead animal wrapped in one of his own t-shirts. Jimmy thought that it was a threat from one of the other kids on the island, since he'd been a target of the local bullies for years. But the description was too close to the one his grandmother 'found' under Sean's bed. She claimed it was placed there by the Grishla as a threat. Ann, his grandmother's former therapist, explained his grandmother had, in fact, created the one under Sean's bed herself, to convince him that the Grishla was real. Later, when Jimmy told him about his situation, Sean figured that his grandma somehow stole one of Jimmy's shirts and created a similar—and gruesome—threat aimed to further inspire Sean's belief in her fictional monster. But Sean told her he'd created a spell to chase the monster off of the island. He thought that was the end of it.

Or was it? He wondered. *Is Jimmy in danger? Could she actually hurt him and claim he was attacked by the Grishla?*

Sean shook off the thought.

No! It has to be a coincidence. It has to be. Stop spooking yourself!

Suddenly, Ann's words entered his mind again.

'*Sean, I'm scared for Gregg Redcrow. I'm afraid your grandmother might hurt him to make it look like the Grishla is real.*'

Chapter Four

Amanda Redcrow turned off the car engine, closed her eyes and prayed for strength. A sob momentarily broke though, but she forced the emotions back down once more. She had to be strong, she needed to do this. It was the only thing she could do for her family now...

Releasing a quivering sigh, she opened the door and exited her rental sedan.

After closing the door, she leaned against the car door, examining the now empty building. Before her stood a ranch-style house that looked like one of the old missions down in California with its brilliant white stucco walls and rustic wood trim. This was the house she grew up in. It was once a place of love, laughter and music, yet now all of the warmth of the building had been siphoned away. This place no longer felt like home. More than that, it radiated an almost sinister air.

A breeze rustled through the bushes, trees, and ferns, otherwise, it was quiet...bleak, unfeeling, stone-cold silent. This place was as dead as her parents.

Dead. She thought. *Everything is dead.*

Another light gust and a torrent of leaves and pine needles blew across the path in front of her. There was a slight chill in the air, and Amanda pulled her sweater tighter around her. A strange feeling of expectation fell across her, a haunting apprehension. Looking around the leaf-littered lawn, Amanda could almost swear she was being watched, and her heart momentarily skipped a beat. Nonetheless, she saw nothing out of place and no movement other than the bushes, trees, and overgrown grass waving in the breeze.

I should just go into the house, she told herself. *What am I waiting for? My father to open the front door? The sound of my mother playing the piano? They're gone, Amanda. They're not coming back.*

But as the odd dread began to build, she realized there was one more person who had been here, someone who was very much still among the living and could still be around.

Her parents' killer.

"Oh god!" she yelped and whirled around to face the gate that led to the street.

There was no one there; she was alone.

Your parents were killed in a road rage incident, Amanda. You have no reason to believe he would come to the house.

More leaves and pine needles blew across the paved path, skittering and scratching their way across the paver stones like angry spiders.

Of course...it did happen just a few hundred yards from the house...on an empty stretch of country road with no traffic and no neighbors...

Amanda turned around and rapidly walked toward the front door, occasionally looking over her shoulder toward the gate. By the time she reached the front porch she'd broken out into a dead run and almost slipped as she clambered up the stone steps. Reaching the door, she fumbled through her purse looking for the keys.

"Damn it, where are the keys?" she grumbled, her eyes occasionally darting back to the front gate. Unreasonable panic clouded her mind as her hand found her wallet, tissues, sunglasses but nothing else. "Why did I just drop them in here when I knew my purse was such a mess...?" Her fingers finally felt the

The Hunted Tribe: Rocket's Red Glare

familiar cold metal, and the sharp edges where the keys had been cut dug into her skin. "Yes!" she, exclaimed as she latched onto them and pulled them out.

She opened the screen door, inserted the spare key her father gave her into the lock and turned it...*click!*

"Oh thank goodness," said Amanda and then exhaled. Her heart felt like it was a runaway horse. Unintentionally, she had spooked herself.

Pushing the door open and walking in, she caught out of the corner of her eyes something black and unfamiliar behind her against the white wall. Startled, Amanda quickly turned around, nearly tripping over her own feet.

"What the heck?" she said, flabbergasted. She reached out and ran her hand along an unfamiliar black panel on the wall. "A security system? Dad, when did you add this?"

Fortunately for her, it had not been turned on. She remembered the police report, her dad had rushed out of the house when he heard the accident. The police probably closed and locked the door when they left, otherwise the door no doubt would have been left wide open.

When I was a kid, we never locked this door. So why the change now? Why a security system? She wondered.

Considering this new addition to the household and how her parents died, she wondered for the first time if their murder had truly been a road rage incident.

Was he scared of someone? Were they being stalked?

***

Sean bit into his sandwich, determined to ignore the concerns that plagued his mind. The sandwich was delicious, of course. The satisfying crunch and blend of spices momentarily made him forget everything else. His grandmother might be losing her mind, but she wasn't losing her touch in the kitchen.

It's fine, Sean. Just calm down. You're going to get your grandmother off her herbal concoctions and get her well enough so that she can take legal custody of you. After that, you will take care of her until you are eighteen, just as you planned, and if she needs to go into a home at that time, you'll make sure she gets into the best place possible.

Sean thought back to his conversation with Ann. She told him to leave the island and get away from his grandmother as fast as he could. But he was torn. He was afraid of going home (his parents had, after all, threatened to put him in a reform school before he left, wrongly believing he had started a fire at the house), and he was also afraid of where his parents would place his grandmother. They didn't care about her the way he did. His mother, in fact, hated his grandmother. Sean knew exactly what his mother would do, too. She'd place his grandmother in the cheapest place she could find, and his father would go along with whatever she said, as always. Sean, being only sixteen years old and a minor, would be powerless to stop them.

In the end, it was Jimmy who helped Sean find a solution he could live with. He suggested that Sean hide the truth from his parents and the world, find a way to stay with his grandmother until he was a legal adult, then get her to sign over legal and medical powers to him. That way he could then ensure whatever the situation, her best interests would be served.

For a moment, Sean glanced up at his friends, silently watching them as they laughed and chatted back and forth. Tom and Bear were the best. He didn't have friends like them back in New York¾or any friends at all, for that matter. But he had decided to hide the truth from them as well as his family. In the end, the only one he truly trusted was Jimmy. It was nothing against the other guys, but he could have never told them about his problems. They were too... normal. They had supportive parents and happy childhoods. They could never understand what it was like for him or Jimmy, unable to trust the adults around them. To Tom and Bear, the very idea of this would be completely alien.

He was so grateful for Tom and Bear's friendship. He truly was. He knew, though, that Jimmy would always be his best friend; he was the only one who really understood how alone Sean felt.

"Really good, huh?" asked Jimmy, breaking Sean's train of thought.

"Yeah, wonderful," said Sean, trying to sound convincing as he pulled himself out of his funk. "I love Mediterranean food."

"Yep, yep, love Mediterranean food, too" repeated Jimmy.

Sean could only smile back. The guy had been a shut in most of his life, trapped in a household with his drunk parents and stuck caring for his two younger siblings. He doubted Jimmy ever had authentic Mediterranean food in his entire life and probably could count the times he'd eaten out at a restaurant on one hand. Sean didn't like to think about all of the things Jimmy had missed out on in his young life.

For a few minutes, the group grew quiet as they enjoyed their lunches. Purple hues began to blend in with the reds and oranges, the colors dancing across both the sky above and the waves below. In the distance, he could hear a band playing and the sound of children laughing. A warm breeze wafted across the water, carrying with it the smell of saltwater and barbeques.

Another perfect night in paradise, thought Sean. *Crazy grandmother and all, this place is the best.* He took another bite of his sandwich. *She's innocent of Gregg Redcrow's death, the death of Gregg's wife, Jimmy...all of it. I know she is.*

Chapter Five

Amanda cautiously entered her father's study, her eyes darting to key areas. The police had been in the house since the murders, but that was several weeks ago. Since then, the house had laid empty and the security system had been turned off, leaving the house vulnerable to an intruder, including the one person that knew no one was coming home—her parents' murderer.

"Okay, it's fine, it's fine," she muttered, placing her hand on her heart, willing it to slow down its rapid gallop.

Everything was where it should be. His expensive computer sat on the desk, and the large-screen television still hung on the wall. Surely, if someone had broken into the home after her parents passed away, they would have taken these items first.

Feeling more confident, she took a step forward and almost tripped over a cardboard box. Amanda caught her balance by grabbing the door frame, but stared bewildered down at the box. It contained her father's plaster casts of the two Dina…Dena…something… footprints. She couldn't remember the name of the dinosaur; they were never really her thing.

Kneeling down next to the box, she pulled out the two casts and found a few other things. A photo album of the family when Amanda was a child, her dad's old Swiss army knife, and his high school ring. From the odd assortment of personal items, it was very clear a thief hadn't packed up this box. Each of these items represented a part of her father's life, a part he would never abandon, but would only be valuable to him. Clearly, he had packed the box.

But why? she wondered. *Why would he do that? They were just coming for a visit, not moving to California...*

Or were they?

Her father said there was something they wanted to discuss with her when they go there, something important. Had they decided to move? And if so, why keep it a secret? Once more, Amanda wondered if they were being stalked by someone.

Taking a second glance in the box, she saw a pad of paper. Amanda reached in and pulled it out, hoping it would provide a clue as to why her father was packing up. On the pad was Elizabeth Wolf's name and under it was a phone number. Below that, he had written out another name Amanda didn't recognize: Sean Wolf. The name Sean Wolf was underlined several times in red.

"Huh," Amanda muttered, trying to remember where she had heard the name. "Elizabeth Wolf's son? No, grandson...that's right."

Amanda stood up and walked over to the desk with the intent of leaving the pad of paper out for her to call the number later. *Perhaps Elizabeth knows what was going on over here,* she thought. But as she reached the desk she stopped, surprised yet again.

On the desk, lying flat, out of its frame and face up, was a photo of her mother and father on their wedding day. On top of the photograph was her father's Revealing Stone, and next to that was a figurine of a rattlesnake. Absentmindedly, her fingers followed the cold, hard form of the figurine, while her mind reflected on the significance.

Amanda's father once told her that the rattlesnake

The Hunted Tribe: Rocket's Red Glare

was an ancient symbol of warning, typically left on the body of a vanquished enemy.

***

"Good day at the pit, right guys?" said Tom, breaking the silence. "I do believe a toast is in order, what do you say?"

The other three nodded, all smiles, and raised their root beers.

Tom cleared his throat, preparing to lead the toast, as always. It was obvious he relished his nickname, 'Fearless Leader', either ignoring or not noticing the sarcasm in the other boys' voices when they called him that.

"When we first found the filled-in pit a few weeks back," started Tom, his voice comically serious, sounding very much like an executive at a board meeting. "We all made jokes about how we had discovered a treasure pit, just like the one they found on Oak Island, 'The Money Pit' as people refer to it. But, when we found the first platform of logs, just like the platform of logs in the Money Pit, we realized we had truly discovered something extraordinary. Well today, gentlemen, we have reached yet another milestone in our adventure¾we've hit the second platform! Cheers to our success!"

The others yipped and cheered, and all drank to the toast.

"And may it be the last one before the treasure!" added Bear.

"I don't think I'd get my hopes up on that one," said Sean. "In the real pit they hit ten platforms."

Tom gasped, then sputtered out: "T...t...ten?!"

Bear gulped and remarked, "That's right you told us that...I forgot..."

"I can't dig down that far," stammered Tom. "Come on guys, it's time to bring in my dad."

"No, no, we can't let adults get involved in this!" cried out Jimmy, a spark of panic igniting behind his eyes. "You know what will happen, they'll just shove us aside and take everything, including the credit."

"No, my dad's not like that. One of the companies he owns is a construction company. He'll bring in heavy equipment..."

"No! We've settled this already," said Sean. "We took a vote¾a fair vote. And we all agreed it would be just us. Besides, this is a smaller scale version, or at least it seems to be. Every five feet we come across a platform, rather than ten feet like the other pit. Maybe the fifth platform will be the last one before the treasure."

"And if it isn't, I say we take another vote," snapped back Tom, crossing his arms across his chest.

After a short pause, the other three finally nodded in agreement, although Sean and Jimmy did so less enthusiastically. They were both in a bad family situation, and their lives would not fare well under close scrutiny. If word got out about their current circumstances, Sean would be shipped back to New York, and Jimmy would end up in Family Services. They both had a lot to lose.

"Let's not talk about this now," said Tom, changing the topic, smoothing back his perfect blonde hair. "Let's talk about what we'll do once we get to the treasure."

Bear laughed. "I thought we all voted for your plan to start a treasure hunting company."

"Yeah, but beyond that! We're going to be rich men. We can't just work all of the time."

"College, I guess," said Bear. "My dad would make me go, rich or not."

"College?" said Jimmy, sitting up. "I...I never thought I'd get to go college."

Sean smiled. *Jimmy probably thought he'd never get to do anything with his life.*

Jimmy's brow furrowed, giving the topic serious consideration, while a hopeful smile spread across his face. "What would I take?"

"Well, what do you want to take?" laughed Tom.

Jimmy shook his head. "I haven't a clue...like I said, I never thought I'd get to go."

His smile suddenly faded, and he leaned back in his chair, disappointment etched on his face. "It's all nonsense. Something will happen. There won't be any treasure or...I don't know...something. I shouldn't even be thinking about this."

"You know, you don't need treasure to go to college," said Bear. "My sister is going on student loans. You could do that."

Jimmy perked up once again. "Really?" He then shook his head and groaned. "Never mind, it doesn't matter. That wouldn't work for me, my parents are dirt poor..," He paused, looked slightly uncomfortable and added, "I think they have bad credit, too. They'd never get approved for a loan."

"It doesn't matter," answered Bear, after taking a long swallow from his can of cola. "When you hit twenty-three it's based on your credit and income... and being poor won't hurt you at all. It will just help you get more grants."

Jimmy's eyes lit up. "Does anyone have a piece of paper?" his voice was excited and urgent now. "I want to write out some ideas!"

Sean reached into his bag and pulled out his journal, then ripped out a few sheets for Jimmy.

"What is that, your diary?" asked Bear.

Sean quickly closed the book and placed it back in his bag. "Yeah. My journal."

"Why would you carry around your journal?" asked Tom.

"I...uh...forgot it was in there," he lied. Sean placed his bag on the ground next to his chair. It took everything he had to lift his hand off the bag and the journal. He wanted so badly to pull out his journal and write in it¾and what he wanted to write was a spell, any spell. His entire being ached for it.

The whole witch thing had been nonsense, Sean knew this. A figment of his grandmother's dementia. There was no Grishla, no Dwanake tribe, all of it had been fake. So why was his grandmother right about him developing a desire to write spells? Was it the power of suggestion? What was wrong with him? Sometimes he felt like a junky, only at least if he was addicted to drugs, that would make some kind of sense. But addicted to writing spells? It was humiliating…and very confusing. The worst part was, his strange addiction seemed to get worse every day.

"Look!" yelled Tom, leaning back in his chair and pointing up at the sky. "The fireworks are starting."

"And the National Anthem," called out Jimmy, enthusiastically jumping to his feet and putting his hand over his heart. "Come on, guys, get up."

The other three exchanged glances. Sean couldn't remember the last time he bothered to stand for the National Anthem.

"Ah, come on, Jimmy," grumbled Bear. "It's not like we're at a ball game or something. Who is going to see us? Who'll care…?"

"I care!" remarked Jimmy. "Where is your national pride?"

Grudgingly, the other three boys got to their feet as well, Bear verbalizing a few grunts of discontent.

As Sean held his hand over his heart, staring at the fireworks and listening to the song, he thought about the lyrics. This was about men fighting for their freedom, declaring war on their oppressors. It seemed so odd listening to it now. Just two weeks ago he thought he was fighting his own war on the Grishla, fighting for the Dwanake's right to live, not knowing if he would live or die. It was all make-believe, sure, but at the time it seemed very real to him. He would never

The Hunted Tribe: Rocket's Red Glare

forget the fear and the nightmares. Never. For the rest of his life, Sean wouldn't be able to listen to this song again and not be moved.

In spite of himself, he felt tears beginning to well up in his eyes. He quickly wiped them away, but then to his complete and utter shock, he heard someone else crying.

Sean turned to look at Jimmy and saw tears running down his freckled cheeks.

"...and the rockets' red glare..," sang Jim slightly off-key along with the song between sniffles.

By now, all of the guys had noticed. They said nothing, but exchanged bewildered glances. Finally, as the song ended, Tom turned to Jimmy and put a hand on his shoulder.

"Gosh, Jimmy, are you okay?" Tom asked.

"Yeah...yeah...sorry," Jimmy's face instantly blushed, and he began to wipe away the tears with the sleeves of his shirt.

"Dude, it's just a song," commented Bear, sounding genuinely concerned.

Jimmy surprised all of them yet again, by whirling around on Bear with fury in his eyes.

"It is not just a song! It's about men going to war, men who would have rather stayed at home and cared for their families and children, forced to kill and be killed! But they did what they had to in order to save their people. You...you can't even imagine the horror of killing when you don't want to...you've never been on a battlefield and heard the plaintive pleas for mercy from your victims..."

"Dude, neither have you!" snapped back Bear. "Have you totally lost it?"

The anger left Jimmy's face, and he looked very sheepish and embarrassed again. "I'm sorry...my uncle went to war and...and..." Jimmy then simply shook his head.

"Was he killed?" asked Tom softly.

"No, it just...destroyed his soul, ate away his mind. Because of his job, he killed a lot of people, and the guilt...well, he never got over it. He volunteers at a church when he has free time, trying to bring some good into this world, but it doesn't stop the nightmares. Worse, he's still in the military, and he's still has to—" Jimmy stopped abruptly and looked away for a moment. No one said a word, they all knew what he meant by this, and an uncomfortable silence followed. After a few brief moments, Jimmy continued, "I'm just saying, it doesn't matter that he was and is fighting for his country, war destroys people's lives. It's hard to understand it if you haven't seen what it does to people. I understand and Sean certainly understands..."

"Umm...I do?" asked Sean, startled. The truth was, he *did* know what it felt like to be caught up in a war, to live in mortal fear, preparing to kill someone else or be killed, making the decision to sacrifice your entire future for the greater good. He also remembered in a drug-induced vision watching the Grishla's victim, feeling their terror as they were robbed of their very lives. It wasn't real, of course. But real or not, he had experienced the emotion with the same intensity. Of course, Jimmy couldn't have known about that. "What makes you think I'd understand anything about war?"

"Your father," said Jimmy. "He was in the war. Didn't you say that?"

"Uh...no, he wasn't," said Sean, as he watched Jimmy make his way toward the steps. Jimmy's movements were stiff, as if he were numb with pain.

"My mistake," muttered Jimmy, descending the stairs, not looking back. "I'll be right back. Just need a minute."

"Bathroom is to your right at the bottom of the stairs," said Tom, watching Jimmy disappear.

"He sure is sensitive, isn't he?" said Bear and the other two nodded in agreement.

Chapter 6

Sean leaned back in his seat as they grew closer to Gregg's house. It was only a half a mile away now. The winding road led them through lush farmland and forest, the kind of which he had only seen on television. It was so beautiful, he wished they had come under better circumstances.

"So this guy studied the Deinonychus!" exclaimed Jimmy, excitedly. "I'm so glad you like dinosaurs too, Sean. It's something more we can talk about!"

Sean nodded. His fragile lie could fall apart if Jimmy asked too many questions. He had told Jimmy that Gregg Redcrow was a friend of his grandmother's, and he was a leading expert on the Deinonychus. The last part was true and enough to get his friend in the car, what with Jimmy's obsession with dinosaurs. But, what he hadn't told him was that they wouldn't be meeting Gregg because he was dead and Sean suspected his grandmother was the one who killed him.

"There!" said Jimmy, sounding like a kid rushing down the stairs on Christmas day. "The dead end sign. We're on the right street!"

The road became steep with several curves. It was a dark road with tall pines and Sean felt a frigid nip in the air as they grew closer, despite it being such a warm summer day.

What do I think I'll find here? Why am I doing this?

As they took another turn around a bend, Jimmy abruptly slowed down the car. "Oh my gosh. Look at that."

A group of trees next to a ditch were burned black. There were skid marks on the road.

This is it, thought Sean. *This is where it happened, this is where Gregg's wife was run off the road.*

"Stop here!" said Sean. "I want to take a look."

Sean expected an argument and was trying to formulate a good reason for wanting to get out of the car, but he soon discovered this wasn't necessary. Jimmy simply nodded and pulled over the car.

Jimmy is beyond any doubt the most easygoing person I have ever met! he thought to himself for probably the hundredth time.

As the car pulled to a stop, Sean jumped out and raced over to the skid marks. They were clearly from a medium-sized truck. The police report said Michelle Redcrow had been driving a truck when she was run off the road and into a ditch just a few hundred yards down the road from their home. Sean stood up, turned and looked down the road. Sure enough, he could see a single mailbox a few hundred yards away, the only one on the entire street. That had to be Gregg's house, and this had to be the accident site.

He briefly looked around, startled by the familiarity of the setting. It really did look exactly like the place he had imagined in his drug-induced trip the night of the campout.

Remembering this night, Sean's chest tightened. *Your grandmother is ill, Sean, it's not her fault,* he told himself once again. Yet he couldn't shake the oppressive feeling that he had been violated.

His grandmother, so determined to make him believe he was a witch had really done a number on him that night. By slipping an exceptionally powerful drug into his food (he shuddered at the thought of what it must have been, certainly something stronger than the herbs she had used other days), Sean's grandmother put him in some kind of trance where he had a vision of the Grishla's victims at the moment of their death. In this case, Sean had imagined he had watched her die in the truck. But how was that possible? He didn't even know about this woman or her death when he had the hallucination. Did his grandmother describe it to him while he was in his drug-induced state?

Isn't it obvious? thought Sean, shaking it off. *It's the Northwest, it's got pine trees and berry bushes. Every place in the Northwest looks alike, so cut it out. Stop trying to convict your grandmother of their murders and start looking for evidence that it was someone—or even something—else.*

Sean directed his eyes to the asphalt, and to his surprise, quickly saw something critical was missing.

"What are you looking at?" asked Jimmy, walking up beside him.

"I'm looking for the other skid marks, from the other truck," said Sean.

"Truck?" asked Jimmy confused, following behind Sean.

"Greg's wife was killed in a hit and run accident," said Sean, as he mentally wondered what the absence of the other skid marks meant, only half paying attention to what he was telling Jimmy. "Her truck was hit in the side by another truck and was thrown into the ditch. It then caught on fire, and she died."

"That's horrible!" gasped Jimmy, stopping dead in his tracks. "Maybe we shouldn't be bothering Gregg Redcrow right now. He must be devastated!"

Sean cringed. "Uh, well..."

Jimmy cocked his head to the side. "Sean? Is there something you're not telling me?"

"Uh...yeah...uh...Gregg is dead too," he finally admitted and saw Jimmy take a step back in shock.

"Then why...why are we...?"

"It's...it's difficult to explain. I'm sorry, I...well, I... oh, to hell with it...I lied."

At first, Jimmy looked upset, even angry. Sean instantly felt sick. This was exactly what he had feared. Then, to his surprise, Jimmy closed his eyes, shook his head, then looked back at Sean and smiled.

"I believe in you, Sean. I know you wouldn't lie if you didn't have a good reason. Just like when I lied to you about my parents being sick, not wanting to tell you the real reason my dad and mom lock themselves away in the house. I know you knew the truth back then, but you kept your mouth shut. I owe you the same trust."

Feeling his face flush in embarrassment, Sean stammered. "I...I can't tell you why I brought you out here...but I swear..."

"When you're ready to tell me the truth you will. For now, let's not worry about it. Just tell me what we need to do next."

Sean stared back at him stunned.

"You're the best friend I've ever had," blurted out Sean. "I mean it, man, you really are!"

Jimmy smiled and returned a half laugh. "You're the best friend I've ever had too. That's why I believe in you. I wouldn't do this for anyone else, not even Bear or Tom."

Sean swallowed hard. Now that the truth was out, he'd have to involve Jimmy further in his plan; he'd need Jimmy to tell a lie now. Sean felt uncomfortable about this. Considering the level of trust Jimmy had just handed him on a silver platter, it felt wrong, felt like he was taking advantage of him. Jimmy deserved better than that, yet still, Sean was desperate. He needed to know if his grandmother was a murderer or not.

"Can I ask one more favor?"

Jimmy nodded enthusiastically. "Sure!"

"Can you pretend like you don't know they're dead? Can you pretend that we both think he's alive, and we're here to see his collection?"

"Sure. I take it that's our goal? To get in the house and see the collection?" asked Jimmy. "Was he really a friend of your grandmother's?"

"Yes. You see, I want to ask his family as much about their connection to my family as possible. And his research. Mostly why he was researching the Deinonychus to begin with."

"Okay," Jimmy answered, rubbing his chin, contemplating the request. "Sounds easy enough and innocent enough. We're just looking for information, right?"

Sean gave an exaggerated nod.

"Well, then let's get back in the car then," he said.

"Oh! One more thing!"

"Another thing?" asked Jimmy, looking nervous now. "We're going to end up in jail, aren't we?"

"No, no, of course not. I just wanted to ask a second favor. If I sneeze, can you excuse yourself to the bathroom so I can talk to his relatives alone? If there are relatives there, that is. I don't know for sure who will be there, if anyone."

"And if there aren't any relatives there, do we go talk to the neighbors or something?"

"No, the neighbors won't know anything. We won't talk to anyone then."

Jimmy looked a little sheepish.

"If no one is there…well, then…um…you're…you're planning on breaking in to see the collection, aren't you?"

Sean swallowed hard.

"I'd like to," said Sean, but then paused. He could see in Jimmy's eyes that this was a deal breaker. He quickly added. "But if we can't get in, we're not going to break in. I wouldn't put you in that situation. What I really need is to speak to the relatives. The collection by itself probably wouldn't tell me much anyway."

"Does this have something to do with the accident?" asked Jimmy, pointing to the burnt trees.

Sean stared back at him blankly, unable to answer. Jimmy was right, of course, but Sean didn't want to explain that part. How could he tell him he suspected his own grandmother of murder?

Jimmy sighed and scratched his head, no doubt figuring out that this question hit the mark, yet for some reason the answer made Sean feel very uncomfortable.

"Okay," said Jimmy, not waiting for an answer. "Let's get back to the car then."

As the two walked back, Sean stopped and knelt down to get a better look at something. He ran his fingers along the black asphalt.

"What is it?" asked Jimmy, pausing as he opened the car door.

"Look...here, here...and here!" Sean said pointing to three areas on the asphalt. "Don't those look like claw marks?"

Jimmy left the car, walked back and knelt down next to Sean, examining the groups of slashes. "Sean, this road has pot holes all over it. I don't know what would make marks like these. It could be anything. Well, anything except an animal. An animal would have to be pretty powerful to leave scratches in asphalt."

Sean nodded but could barely keep his eyes off the marks.

A normal animal couldn't make these kind of tracks, but what about a dinosaur animal spirit? One powerful enough to throw a truck into a ditch? A tingle of excitement danced across his skin. He so wanted the Grishla to be real now. It was absurd, but he'd rather be stalked by an animal spirit than know his grandmother was a murderer.

Another thought then entered his mind, and he felt

his heart rate quicken. *If the Grishla was real, I drove it off the island with my spell. Well...I'm off the island now, too. Wouldn't the creature use this to its advantage? Kill me while I'm off the island and vulnerable?*

Sean quickly stood back up and examined the trees around him. An odd insect hum permeated the trees and bushes around him. It was strange and creepy, not helping to settle his jangled nerves. But not surprisingly, nothing around them moved, there were no sounds of footsteps or anything even slightly suspicious.

You're spooking yourself, Sean. Cut it out!

"Let's get going," said Sean, and the two returned to the car and began to climb in.

Snap!

Sean jumped back from the car and whirled around as he heard something moving in the trees across the road from the car.

"What's wrong now?" asked Jimmy.

Snap, crunch, snap...

"There's something in the woods!" gasped Sean, backing up until his back struck the car. "It's coming towards us!"

"So?" asked Jimmy.

Suddenly, the creature immerged. Not a dinosaur as Sean had though, but something with a long, menacing snout and pointed, brown ears. The thing then stood up, straight up like a man. It towered over Sean and looked down at him with disdain. The snout...the long ears...the gangly limbs...the creature was unmistakable.

A werewolf? Thought Sean. *A WEREWOLF!???*

"Run, Jimmy, run!" yelled Sean, ready to take flight himself. He turned and only saw a perplexed expression on his friend's face.

"What?" asked Jimmy, leaning against the car and staring at Sean as if he thought he were insane. "Why in the world would I run?"

Snort! Snort!

Sean turned back around to face the monster. The werewolf grunted, then dropped to all fours. It then looked up at Sean with a pair of big, soulful doe eyes. Two fawns came out of the woods behind it and also looked up him with a wariness.

A deer…it was only a deer…

"Son of a..," gasped Sean, practically falling back against the car. Fury then took over, and he began to walk toward the deer, waving his arms in the air. "Get out of here! Go away! Go away!"

Startled, the doe and her fawns darted back into the forest, effortlessly bounding over bushes and rocks until they disappeared among the trees.

"Why'd the heck did you do that?" asked Jimmy, shocked. "You scared them!"

"I scared them?!" snapped back Sean, wiping the sweat from his forehead. "Why the heck was that deer standing up like that? I didn't even know they could do that!"

Jimmy casually shrugged. "They do it sometimes to make themselves look bigger and scare off predators."

"Well, it worked!" returned Sean, his hands still shaking. "My heart nearly exploded from my chest! I thought it was a werewolf!"

"A werewolf?" gasped Jimmy. "Hahahahahahahaha!!!!"

Anger began to bubble inside of Sean, but then he thought about how ridiculous the whole situation was, telling his friend to run for his life over a momma doe and her two baby fawns, and he began to laugh as well.

I know, whispered the sinister voice of Hugo the Jerk in his ear. *Tell him what you really thought, that it was a dinosaur animal spirit come to get yah!*

"Oh, gosh, how has my life come to this?" said Sean between the laughter.

Chapter 7

The car barely drove another hundred yards until they reached the mail box Sean had seen from the accident site. Behind the mailbox on the gate was a sign marked "Redcrow Ranch, Private Property." Jimmy turned up the driveway and headed toward the house.

A car was parked outside the house, and Sean felt a spark of hope. Maybe it was the surviving daughter?

Sure enough, a twenty-something woman stepped out on the porch and looked at them as they drove up.

"You do the talking, Mr. Slimy Conman," snickered Jimmy. "I'm just the getaway driver."

Sean laughed and shook his head. "I'll just tell her we were driving up from California to visit my grandmother and wanted to visit Gregg. With a little luck, she'll invite us into the house. Remember, we don't know he's dead."

"Right," answered Jimmy.

Sean opened the car door, got out of the car and waved at the woman.

"Good morning!" he said enthusiastically.

She returned a short nod but gave him a wary look.

Sean walked toward the gate separating the driveway from the front yard, and walked toward the woman and extended his hand. "Hi, I'm looking for Gregg Redcrow's house. I'm Sean Wolf, Elizabeth Wolf's grandson."

The woman's eyes grew wide with surprise, then she seemed to recover and continued. "I'm Amanda Redcrow, Gregg's daughter. And you're Sean Wolf, you say? I just got off the phone with your grandmother. She told me you were up in the San Juan Islands, Elk Island, if I'm not mistaken, visiting her. What are you doing way down here?"

"Ummm..," started Sean.

If she spoke with my grandmother, he thought to himself, *then she must know that I know Gregg is dead. So there goes my plan...I can't tell her I was just stopping by to visit with him and see his dinosaur artifact collection when I already knew he was dead. What do I say? What do I say?*

To his horror, Sean felt the gears in his brain shutting down. He continued to stare back at her blankly.

"Sean?" asked Amanda

Beads of sweat broke out across his brow. He couldn't think of a single word to say.

"Sean?" asked Amanda again.

Sean's head began to throb. *Do something! Say something, you idiot!* His mind screamed, yet still nothing came.

"Hi, my name is Jimmy Cooper," said Jimmy, walking around the front of the car. "We're really sorry to come without calling. But don't blame Sean, it was my idea. Yeah, it was my idea. I just...I..." He hung his head on this last comment as though he was too sad to go on.

What is he doing? thought Sean. *He's a terrible liar! He's going to get us caught!*

As he watched Jimmy, however, even he was starting to feel convinced. He looked absolutely miserable.

"Oh, it's fine, it's fine," said the woman, rushing over to Jimmy and putting her hand on his shoulder. "I was just surprised, please tell me."

"Gosh, I feel so terrible!" exclaimed Jimmy, still looking down at the ground. "Gregg wanted to show Sean his collection and had even invited me along. What a great guy, he didn't even know me, but just because I said I liked dinosaurs he included me. When I talked to Gregg on the phone he was so excited to show us his collection—*so excited!*—and I put off the trip because I was so busy. I thought we had all the time in the world..." He began to pace and rub his temple as if he was terribly upset. "I could tell his collection was his pride and joy, and all he wanted was for us to see it, and I couldn't make the time. It was such a simple request and it seemed so important to Gregg at the time. I feel terrible, just terrible! Why didn't I just make the time? Why?"

Tears seemed to be welling up in Jimmy's eyes, as he coyly wiped at his eyes.

Okay, now this act is just a little too good, thought Sean, stunned. *Where did this Oscar-winning performance come from?*

"Oh, don't feel bad," she said, her mothering instinct clearly kicking in. "You had no way of knowing this was going to happen."

"No, I didn't, but it's too late now," continued Jimmy, his voice cracking. "That's why we came up. I just wanted to apologize to his family...I just wanted to tell them I'm so, so sorry..."

Amanda, now completely overwhelmed by his performance, pulled Jimmy into a hug. "Oh, honey, it's okay, it's okay!"

Jimmy continued to put on his performance, sniffling and trembling in her arms like a five-year-old child. Sean, nearly forgetting himself, crossed his arms in disgust.

Holy freakin' cow, he thought. *Talk about over the top.*

Amanda pulled back and looked intently at Jimmy. "You know what? You're right, my father's collection was his pride and joy. It would be my honor to show it to both of you now. We can look at it in his memory, what do you say?"

Jimmy smiled weakly and nodded. "We would like that very much. I know wherever Gregg is, he will be looking down at us and smiling. Let's honor his memory. Yes, yes, indeed, let's honor his memory."

Amanda motioned for them to follow her into the house. As she turned her back to them, Jimmy's sad face abruptly dropped, and he gave Sean a victorious smile and a wink.

Once again, Sean was floored. *Who is this guy and where is my shy friend?*

Then he smiled and realized the truth: Jimmy had grown since he first met him. Before, Jimmy was alone in the world, the kid who was always being picked on by the local bullies. Now, he had friends and nobody dared to bother Jimmy in front of the other guys. Their friendship with him had given him what he needed to evolve into a confident, happy human being.

Still, thought Sean to himself. *This is a huge change. I really didn't think it was possible for him to change this much in the past few weeks.*

They followed Amanda into a house that looked like an old Spanish mission. White walls, ancient terracotta tiles on the floor, and a large wrought iron cross on the wall. They continued down the hall until they reached a room with glass cases lining the walls.

"Wow!" gasped Jimmy with wide eyes, walking directly toward a collection of footprints on the wall. He abruptly looked down and pointed to two plaster footprints on the side table below the table, sitting next to a small, engraved stone. "Look at these two dinosaur footprints. I think they are each from a Deinonychus, right?"

Amanda smiled and nodded, walking up to the wall. "That's very good. Yes, a large one and a smaller one. Although..," she paused as though unsure if she wanted to tell him the next thing. Finally, shaking her head and laughing, she added. "Actually, my father said the larger print was from a dinosaur animal spirit called the Grishla."

On hearing this, Sean had to suppress a gasp. *So the legend of the Grishla is real? Of course, a legend doesn't mean the creature itself existed.* Still, he could barely believe she actually said the name.

"Really?" said Jimmy. His eyes were practically spinning in his head now from excitement. He didn't know about the Grishla legend, but anything about a dinosaur was enough to get him going. "I've never heard of a Grishla before. And it's a dinosaur animal spirit? That's totally awesome! Why aren't they mounted?"

Amanda shrugged. "My father was going on a trip, to see me actually, and for some reason he had decided to pack them up and take them with him. I don't know why. Anyway, I put them back with the rest for now. I suppose I'll have to pack them all up eventually, or I may mount them back on the wall and keep the house in honor of my parents. Maybe even move up here, not sure, haven't decided yet."

"What's that?" asked Sean, pointing to the engraved stone next to the plaster casts. He suspected he knew, but wanted to hear it from her.

She reached down and picked up the stone. "This is the infamous Revealing Stone. You see, legend has it that the Grishla, as well as all other animal spirits, can take human form. Supposedly, the Revealing Stone forces an animal spirit to change back into its true form. So, if you suspected a friend or family member was in fact the Grishla, you could test it out by having them touch the stone. If they didn't change, they were not an animal spirit."

She extended her hand, offering the stone to Jimmy.

"What an interesting legend," said Jimmy, staring down at the stone.

To Sean's surprise, Jimmy did not take the stone, and instead turned away from it and walked toward another glass case on the wall.

Amanda seemed baffled by Jimmy's behavior as was Sean.

Too many things to see, I guess, thought Sean. *The guy is like a kid in a candy shop.*

"Can I see it?" asked Sean quickly, stepping forward.

"Oh, of course," said Amanda, turning around and handing the stone to him.

Sean stared down at it for a moment. The stone wasn't very impressive. Dull, flat, with a few symbols etched into it. It looked fairly pathetic actually.

"Very nice," returned Sean, not able to think of anything else to say.

I think it's time I spoke to her alone, Sean decided. *I need to get rid of Jimmy. I just hope he remembers the code for him to leave the room. I guess we'll see.*

Sean gave an exaggerated sneeze. "Excuse me!"

"God bless you, Sean," said Jimmy, who then turned to Amanda and asked. "Could I use your restroom?"

She nodded and pointed out the door. "Down the hall, first door on your left."

Jimmy smiled, gave a curt nod, then walked out of the room.

"So...um..," started Sean clumsily. "I was hoping to ask you a few questions."

"Shoot," said Amanda, with a friendly smile.

Here goes looking like a lunatic.

"You know about the Grishla...so I'm assuming... well...your family is part of the Dwanake tribe, right?" he asked tentatively.

The response he received was exactly what he had feared. "Dwa...nak...I'm sorry, I've never heard of them before. Besides, I'm half Sioux and half Cherokee. Sorry."

"My misunderstanding, sorry."

Sean felt his heart sink, but knew already what his grandmother would have said to this: "Some tribe members don't tell their children about their heritage and the curse, wanting them to live a life free of fear."

She really thought out every angle, didn't she?

For a long time, Amanda continued her tour, showing Sean the vast array of footprints her father had collected over the years. Sean had come so far, and now he couldn't seem to think of what to ask. Finally, as they reached Gregg's books, Sean found his voice again.

"At the risk of sounding insensitive, can you tell me about the car accident? I mean…what happened?"

Amanda sighed. "Road rage incident, the police think. First, someone ran my mother's truck off the road. Right up the street, in fact. But, when my father rushed out of the house to her rescue, the jerk knifed him, then drove off. I still can't believe something like this could happen here. In an instant that…monster…robbed me of my parents. I…"

Tears welled up in her eyes, and Sean felt ill that he'd dragged up these terrible memories for her. But he couldn't stop now.

"I'm so sorry. Gosh, how awful! Did they find the guy, I hope?"

She shook her head. "No. They didn't find anything. Not even the tire tracks from the guy's car."

Sean froze at these words. "Isn't that…I don't know…unusual?"

"I don't know," said Amanda, shaking her head and sounding sad and tired. "I don't know."

Jimmy re-entered the room just then, a broad smile on his face. Then, as he saw the expression on Amanda's face, his smile fell.

"We shouldn't be here," said Jimmy, shaking his head. "Nope, nope. We shouldn't be here."

"No, no, it's fine," said Amanda, wiping her eyes.

"No, it isn't fine," stated Jimmy firmly, shooting a

harsh glance at Sean. "We'll be leaving now. Thank you for your patience."

Amanda nodded, and the three walked out of the office. All were silent, each one deep in their own thoughts. What had started out well enough had turned into a very awkward moment. Sean was glad they were leaving now. He got some of his questions answered. His grandmother had indeed made the whole thing up. Even if the Grishla existed in legend, the Dwanake clearly didn't exist in any way, shape or form. No Dwanake...no curse. His grandmother had made up the whole story.

But did she kill Gregg and his wife? That one piece remained shrouded in mystery...and it was the one piece he needed answered above all else.

The three reached the front door, and as Sean reached for the door handle, Jimmy suddenly gasped.

"Oh my gosh, my car keys!" he said, feeling around in his pockets. He then turned toward the study. "I put them on the back table when I was looking at the footprints. That's right. I'll just go grab them."

Amanda nodded and Jimmy ran back into the study.

"So how much further do you have to drive?" asked Amanda, turning to Sean.

***

Jimmy entered the study and walked directly to the back table under the footprints. Sure enough, his keys were lying on the back table. Once he picked them up, he carefully looked back at the door. No one was there. He then placed the keys into his pocket and reached for the Revealing Stone. For a moment, he hesitated, his hand just inches from the rock. Then, finally, he reached down and picked it up, closing his eyes. Jimmy waited a brief moment, then looked down at his arms and legs. With a brief laugh, he placed the stone back down on the table.

"So I'm not an animal spirit. Well how about that? A pity, though. I would have liked to have been an animal spirit, then I could have met up with the Eagle animal spirit, the Wolf animal spirit and...and whatever other animal spirits there are...and we could have had tea or coffee. Maybe we could have started a club or some special council, act as advisors to the other species or something. Darn it. I would have enjoyed that. Yep, would have enjoyed that."

Jimmy turned and walked back to the door to meet up with Sean.

Chapter Eight

Sean stared out the window, watching the same lush farmland and forest pass by as before, yet now he could no longer appreciate it. He felt so much worse now compared to when they had arrived. The entire outing had been a complete bust. Worse, now he questioned his own motives for the trip.

I wasn't there to find out if my grandmother killed Gregg, thought Sean. *I was there to prove the Grishla did it!*

This had to be the case, he decided; after all, he didn't ask one question about his grandmother's relationship with Gregg. Did they like each other, hate each other? And why did Amanda happen to call his grandmother right before they arrive? Did she suspect her grandmother of something? But no, instead Sean only asked questions that would validate his grandmother's insane fantasy—was he part of the Dwanake tribe and were they being hunted by a creature called the Grishla? Any question that might implicate his grandmother he had completely avoided.

Inadvertently, Sean let out a soft chuckle, amused at his own desperate desire to prove his grandmother's sanity. Even though doing so equated to him having a fight to the death with a dinosaur animal spirit.

"What's so funny?" asked Jimmy.

Sean jumped, startled. He had been so wrapped up in his own thoughts, he'd forgotten that Jimmy was sitting right there next to him.

"Nothing," said Sean quickly, trying to sound sincere.

The result wasn't what he had hoped for. Jimmy bowed his head slightly and looked sad.

"I understand," said Jimmy, keeping his eyes focused on the road. "I said I would understand if you didn't tell me, and I do. But...is there a reason you don't trust me? You don't think I'd laugh at you or betray you or something, do you?"

"No, of course not," started Sean, feeling a twinge of guilt now.

Reconsidering this for a moment, he thought, *well maybe laugh...he did laugh at me over that whole werewolf thing.*

"...because," continued Jimmy, "I came a long way out here, driving illegally with no driver's license—which I told you before we left—because I trusted you. So again, I hope this isn't about you not trusting me. I'd be really hurt if that were the case. Yes, really, really hurt if that were the case."

"I trust you, I promise you," replied Sean.

"Good," muttered back Jimmy.

The two sat in silence for a long moment. Then, suddenly, Jimmy spoke up again.

"So? Why aren't you telling me then? You can *at least* tell me that much, right?"

Sean sighed. Jimmy wasn't going to let this go. But did it really matter if Jimmy knew the truth? He already knew Sean's grandmother had severe dementia. And perhaps if he talked it out with Jimmy, he'd help prove his grandmother's innocence?

"Okay, okay, I'll tell you everything" he started, then paused not sure how to start.

A few more seconds passed, and Jimmy continued to glance at Sean expectantly.

"I'm waiting," said Jimmy finally, the fingers of his right hand drumming the car steering wheel.

The Hunted Tribe: Rocket's Red Glare

"I think…I think…I think my grandmother might have…that she might have killed Gregg and his wife."

"WHAT!?"

Distracted by the shocking announcement, Jimmy almost missed the turn and jerked the steering wheel hard to the right. Having to compensate for his overcorrection, he then jerked the wheel hard to the left.

Sean grabbed onto the door as he pitched one direction then another, his seat belt digging into his shoulder. As the car began to bounce, he realized they had actually veered off into a field. A low-hanging tree limb smacked the windshield, and Sean yelped. Finally, after a few terrifying seconds, the bouncing stopped, and he felt the reassuring firmness of the asphalt under the tires. The car was back on the road. Sean's hand, which was now gripping the dashboard in pure fright, relaxed and fell back to his lap.

"Sorry, sorry," muttered Jimmy.

"Would you calm down?"

"No! Tell me more about this bizarre idea you've picked up. I need to know…"

"I'm not telling you anything until you swear you'll calm down!" snapped back Sean, now fearing for his life.

"I promise, I promise," returned Jimmy. Then with a slight growl of frustration, he pointed forward and said, "Look, straight stretch now, no more curves in the road for a while. Just tell me what's going on, and why you would think such a terrible thing."

For the next few minutes, Sean laid out the entire story to Jimmy: Sean being accused of witchcraft by his parents, his grandmother saying he was an Ultra-Witch sent to battle the Grishla, and about how Ann told him that his grandmother was insane. To Jimmy's credit, he quietly nodded without interruption, only raising his eyebrows on a few of the stranger parts. Finally, when Sean finished, he sat back and waited for his friend's reaction.

Hopefully, we'll stay on the road this time, he thought to himself.

"So, if I've got this right," said Jimmy, carefully, keeping his voice steady. "You're not thinking your grandmother accidentally hit Gregg's wife's truck with her jeep, but that she actually deliberately murdered both of them to convince you this Gristle thing is real."

"Grishla," corrected Sean. "And, well…ummm…"

"No, don't you get wishy-washy on me now," said Jimmy sternly. "We came all this way out here so you may as well just grow a backbone and spit it out."

Startled by his friend's confrontational tone, Sean quickly replied, "Yes. You're right. That's why I came out here."

Jimmy shook his head, his mouth pulling down into a frown. "Stupid, idiot kid."

"Hey!" snapped back Sean. This was way over the top now.

"Listen up and listen good," said Jimmy, sounding oddly like Sean's dad more and more by the minute. "It takes a lot of force to slam a truck into a ditch and rupture its gas tank, let alone make it erupt into flames. Does your grandmother's jeep have any damage?"

For a second, Sean felt his heart stop. He hadn't even thought of that.

"No!" he replied excitedly, feeling relief wash over him. But the feeling was short-lived as another idea entered his mind. "Of course, she could have rented a car…"

"Well, that would be a real hoot, now wouldn't it?" remarked Jimmy, in an almost snide voice. Now he really did sound like his dad. "How would you turn in a rental car in that condition? Did you consider that? I mean, they'd ask for a police report, right? Or maybe she didn't return it, maybe she ditched it like the common criminal that she is. The rental car agency, that is no doubt within driving distance of the accident,

The Hunted Tribe: Rocket's Red Glare

would report a car stolen—guess it would have to be truck really to cause that kind of damage—and the police wouldn't make a connection? And what about the credit card she used to rent the car? If she didn't turn in the truck, the police could have easily tracked her down through her credit card."

"Well, maybe she used cash..," started Sean, but was cut off when Jimmy yet again growled.

"Stupid, idiot kid," said Jimmy once more.

"Cut that out!" said Sean. "You're my age, you can't call me a kid…"

"They don't let you rent a car using cash," interrupted Jimmy. "You have to have a credit card."

"How in the hell would you know?"

"I just do," responded Jimmy. "Everybody knows that. Or least I thought everybody knew this, especially some worldly kid from New York City like you. I'm sorry, but exactly how stupid do you have to be not to know that?"

"Hey!!"

"Back on topic, back to your grandmother's geriatric murder caper," said Jimmy forcefully, his eyes flaring as his fury seemed to be growing. "As I said before, they'd use the credit card to track her down. Or maybe your grandmother steals credit cards on the side, too? Oh wait, wait! I've got it! You're sweet little old granny, with the distinguished, silver streaks in her hair, who spends her days rocking in her rocking chair, knitting socks for the homeless, hot-wired a car. That's it! Yeah, I can see it all now!"

"What? She doesn't spend her days in a rocking chair. And hotwire? No…I didn't think…I..," stammered Sean, he then shook his head hard and turned to glare at Jimmy. "What's wrong with you? We're talking about my grandmother, not yours! Why are you getting so mad at me?"

"Because I like your grandmother, okay?" snapped back Jimmy. "Ever since that day she hit me over the head with that shovel, I knew she had spunk. She deserves far better from you than..."

"She hit you over the head with a shovel?" interrupted Sean, astonished at where this conversation had taken them. "When did this happen? And if she hit you in the head with a shovel, why aren't you dead?"

Jimmy sighed and shrugged.

"Alright, alright, maybe it wasn't a shovel, maybe it was a broom or something. But it hurt! I was just a little kid at the time after all."

Sean continued to stare dumbfounded at Jimmy, who let out another deep sigh.

"I got into her garden, and she swatted me with something. Bopped me on the head and told me to get out. It was so spirited, like a noble warrior..."

"A noble warrior? Attacking a little kid with a broom?" said Sean with a laugh. "Yeah, that sounds really noble."

Jimmy shot him a dirty look and continued, "Anyway...I kind of developed a crush on her after that." He paused momentarily, noticing the horrified look on Sean's face. "I don't anymore. I just...I like her. And no matter what you say, I will never believe in a million years that she ever hurt anyone—except maybe me, and I had it coming. Besides, where were you when she disappeared? Maybe you were the one who did it!"

"What?!" yelled Sean, thinking back to how Hugo the Jerk had suggested the same thing earlier. The thought of it still gave him the creeps.

"I like your grandmother," Jimmy repeated again. "If you even think about calling in the police on her, I'll punch you in the nose, you got it?"

"So much for your 'why-don't-you-think-you-can-trust-me-and-why-won't-you-tell-me-what's-going-on?' lecture," responded Sean, crossing his arms over his chest. "Ask me that question again, why don't you? Because I've got a beauty of an answer for you now!"

Jimmy smirked. "Sorry."

Sean shrugged and the two remained quiet for a while. In the silence, Sean continued to contemplate what Jimmy had said. He was right. If Sean had just considered all of the facts, he would have known from day one that his grandmother was innocent. Jimmy was right; Sean was a stupid, idiot kid.

Finally, Sean said, "The police are probably right, it was just a hit and run. Coincidences happen."

"Yep," said Jimmy. "Coincidences happen."

Again, dead silence.

"Look, thanks, you're right of course. Thanks for helping me clear this up in my head—"

"We've got to get home," interrupted Jimmy, still apparently a little angry with Sean. "We've got to get to work on that stupid pit again tomorrow. Three more levels. Why'd you have to go and make it five full levels, Sean? Why not four levels or three?"

"I didn't make it five levels," said Sean. "You make it sound like I created the pit. I just said it was likely…"

Jimmy growled once more, and Sean leaned toward his window, away from Jimmy.

This is going to be a long drive home, Sean thought to himself. But at least it's over now. *At least I know my grandmother isn't a murderer. There wasn't even a murder at all. Everything is fine and always was fine.*

***

In the shadows of a dark room, Ann continued to lie on the twin bed decomposing. Flies walked along the clear plastic that now covered the woman. Through the plastic zip bag, the scent was very slight, certainly not enough to attract the attention of any humans. The flies, however, could not be fooled. They knew when a rotting corpse was near.

Chapter Nine

Sean and Jimmy's drive home did turn out to be very tense and unpleasant, but over the next few weeks, it was as if Jimmy didn't even remember the conversation. Everything else quieted down for Sean as well. With his grandmother no longer using her hallucinogens in his food, he no longer dreamed about Srinam, and Hugo and Richard eventually disappeared completely. The downside of this, of course, was that it allowed Sean time to think about his other problems.

It was August now—summer was drawing to a close. What would his parents decide? Put him in reform school or let him continue in his old high school? Either way, it meant leaving the island, something he didn't want to do. His grandmother said she was working on his parents and told him not to discuss it with them. Leaving him nothing to do but worry—and continue to work on the pit.

Perhaps Jimmy was right to be angry with him for saying there would be five platforms. It really was as if Sean had jinxed them with this comment. They had just passed the fourth platform and still no end in sight. Or perhaps the treasure was just a few scoops of dirt away. It didn't have to be like the Money Pit on Oak Island, with the final platform booby-trapped and a plaque written in a cryptic ancient language sitting on top. Yet he still believed that was what they would find. Silly of him, really.

Pacing in his room now, he looked at the clock: Ten pm. It was getting pretty late, but he was too wound up to sleep. He looked at his journal on his desk, enticing him, begging him to write in it. Why did this strange impulse continued? Why was he completely addicted to writing curses in his journal? It didn't matter, he refused to give in to it. Sean picked up the journal and tossed it into his backpack.

On the table under the window, Sean could see his witchcraft exercise tools, neglected and unused; it had been a good two months since he had touched either of them. On a whim, he picked up the pad of paper, carried it over to his desk and dropped it down.

In a sing-song voice that mimicked the old nursery rhyme *Mirror, Mirror on the Wall*, Sean said, "Pad of paper on the desk. Who's the biggest liar here, I can guess."

He laughed at his joke—it almost rhymed.

Picking up a pen and sitting in the chair, he decided to give the pad of paper another go. He vaguely remembered the previous time he used it, the pad of paper said that magic wasn't real and the legend of the Grishla was a lie. He couldn't quite remember the question he had asked it now, though. Not that it mattered. He wanted to ask it something different. But what?

Setting the tip of the pen on the white paper, Sean closed his eyes and focused. "Oh mystical pad of paper, if the Grishla doesn't exist like you say, who killed Gregg Redcrow and his wife?"

The pen jerked into motion, speeding across the white paper. Unable to stop himself, he began to laugh. He knew psychiatrists called this 'automatic writing', and what was happening was his hand was just writing out his thoughts, buried deep in his own subconscious mind. Still, it felt so strange, like someone else was moving his hand across the pad. It was really bizarre.

The pen abruptly stopped, he involuntarily lifted up

his hand, and the pen clattered to the table. Satisfied it was finished, Sean opened his eyes.

"Ahh!" he yelled, leaping to his feet and stumbling back, almost tripping over the chair he had been previously sitting in as he stared down at the words.

It read: "The Grishla killed Gregg Redcrow and his wife. I never said the Grishla didn't exist, only that the legend was a lie. You really need to start practicing your witchcraft and fast or you and everything you love will die."

Without thinking, Sean grabbed the pad of paper and flung it to the back table, where it slid to the far end and fell between the wall and the table edge, eventually tumbling to the floor in a flutter of pages. With some satisfaction, Sean noted that it landed on its edge with a blank sheet showing, the offending words hidden from sight.

"You're tired, Sean; just too much work and too much worry," he muttered to himself, rubbing his eyes.

***

Early morning light streamed through his window as Sean tied his shoes. Another bright and shiny day, and he was so relieved to get out of the house.

I need to get my mind on other things, he thought to himself. *I need to focus on normal things like hanging out with the guys. I'm starting to lose it.*

He could still see the pad of paper under the table, lying on the floor, mocking him. He'd throw it out, but the truth was he was afraid to touch it. Slowly it dawned on him, something didn't look quite right about the pad of paper. He would have sworn when the pad of paper landed on the floor the previous night, only a blank sheet of white paper showed. However, now the pad had writing on it. Curiosity took hold and he got up and walked toward it, leaning down a bit to see which page was showing. Only one single sentence showed: "You're almost out of time."

He jerked up and stumbled back to the bed, sitting down hard, nearly missing the mattress. *I didn't write that! I NEVER wrote that!* His heart pounding like a jackhammer now, he rubbed his chest, trying to get his over-active organ to calm down.

Sean thought he was past all of the weirdness, but now, for his mind to manufacture such a bizarre message—was his grandmother putting hallucinogenic herbs in his food again?

That's all I need right now...with my luck, my mom will want to give me a drug test and...well, I don't even want to think how she would react if it came back positive...

There was a knock on his bedroom door.

"Come on in," called out Sean.

To his surprise, it was his grandmother carrying none other than the infamous pink bottle of herbs, the one she used to keep her hallucinogenic herbs in—at least before Sean replaced them with Italian herbs.

His grandmother walked over to the bed and sat down next to him, shaking the bottle.

"You know," she started slowly. "I thought all my food tasted funny lately, but it wasn't until I made a batch of chocolate chip cookies and they ended up tasting like lasagna that I finally figured out what was wrong."

She shook her bottle of herbs again.

"I think you need to explain yourself, young man," she said, giving him a stern glare. "Why did you throw out my special spice mix?"

Sean sighed. He'd had enough. It was as simple as that.

He wanted to help her, wanted to protect her, but he wasn't going to spend the rest of his life being poisoned by her, either.

Sean turned to her, returning what he hoped was an

The Hunted Tribe: Rocket's Red Glare

equally stern glare.

"I guess I was just tired of being strung out like a junkie," he replied firmly.

His answer seemed to take her aback for a moment. She blinked hard, sat up straighter, but as she opened her mouth to speak, Sean held up his hand.

"Grandma, I'm the Ultra-Witch," Sean replied sternly. Maybe he could put a stop to this while allowing her to maintain her little fantasy. "When I started feeling bad and seeing…well, things I shouldn't have been seeing…I did a spell and found out you've been doping my food with herbs to increase my magical powers. Am I correct?"

Elizabeth looked astonished, but then nodded. "Yes…well, yes, but…I was only trying to help…"

Sean nodded vigorously. Out of all the insanity he'd been forced to deal with lately, the one thing he was certain of that she was, indeed, only trying to help.

"I know that, I'm not mad. But this stuff is making me sick, and they don't help my magic, they're screwing it up. My practice sessions are much better now, I'm much more effective."

Elizabeth huffed and crossed her arms over her chest. "As if I would know. You never let me watch."

"We've discussed this before," he said. "The magic I use is far too dangerous for you to be around. It's powerful, deadly stuff. And you've seen the results, right? There's not been a single Grishla attack since I started casting my spells, has there?"

She broke into a smile that seemed to shine from her face. "No, there hasn't. The first time in…I don't know how many centuries—the Grishla has simply vanished!" She reached out and took his hand in hers. "Sean, I am so very proud of you!"

Sean smiled back. If only getting rid of an imaginary dinosaur spirit was enough to satisfy his mom and dad, his life would be perfect.

"But no more magic herbs, right? They're messing

me up. And I'm hoping you're not taking them either; Grandma, they're bad news."

Looking down at the pink bottle, she sighed. "They are bad news, more than you know."

Sean looked from the pink bottle to her. That sounded very ominous. He felt a creeping sensation pass through him.

Is there more going on with these herbs? He wondered. *I'm not sure how much more of this I can take.*

Elizabeth closed her eyes as if she were trying to build her strength. Sean then noticed her hands. They were balled into fists and trembling violently. *This is going to be big,* thought Sean, and acid rose into his throat. Suddenly, her eyes popped open, and she looked at him square on, a very serious expression on her face. *Oh…yeah…this can't be good..,* he thought.

"Sean, there's something you need to know," said Elizabeth, sounding as if it took every ounce of courage she possessed to say what she had to tell him. "And I hope…I hope someday you can forgive me…"

On the last couple words, Elizabeth's voice cracked, and Sean thought he was going to be ill, now knowing what she was going to say.

She killed Gregg! No, I don't want to know this! I don't want to know this!!

"You weren't sick as a child," she said finally in a half sob. "Oh, honey, I'd give anything in the world not to tell you this!"

Her face was so grave, Sean wondered if he had misheard her. What she was saying made no sense. It was like asking someone how many fingers you were holding up and having them answer "blue."

Where in the world did this come from? Of course I was sick as a child, I had cancer! I spent most of my life in and out of hospitals getting skin-graphs, bone marrow transplants, chemotherapy, of course, I was sick!

"You see, all of it was...a magic enhancer...like this," she said, holding up the pink bottle. "Your doctor was a member of the Dwanake tribe, a Trebor like myself. When marrying Trebor to Trebor didn't work to create an Ultra-Witch, we used experiments. Skin grafts and bone marrow transplants from powerful Trebors to attempt to increase your power. They were cruel, horrible experiments, but we had no choice! Your sister, your father, your two, dear, sweet cousins who died..." she momentarily stopped as a she clasped her hand over her mouth and let out a tortured sob. "We were trying to save our tribe. You do understand why we did it, don't you, Sean? Please tell me you understand!"

I can't believe how complex her fantasy has become, he thought, dumbfounded by both the scope and detail of this new confession. As she stared back at him expectantly, tears starting to flow down her cheeks. He realized that this was very real to her, and he needed to diffuse the situation right away.

"It's okay, grandma, I know," he said with somber nod. "I saw it with one of my spells. It had to happen. I felt it in my heart. Don't blame yourself anymore."

Elizabeth pulled Sean into a hug, and he hugged her back, his heart breaking as she openly sobbed.

Dementia is such a horrible thing, he thought to himself, wiping away his own tears.

***

The flies trapped in Ann's body bag flew away as the zipper was drawn back. Her killer pulled the plastic away from Ann's head and looked intently down at her decayed face. The smell was intoxicating —delicious.

It was almost time, time for the hunt to begin. A small taste of the last victim was just the ticket needed to build strength, to prepare.

Soon—very soon—the true war would begin.
It had been such a long wait.

Chapter Ten

Dear Diary,

I'm worried about my grandmother. Her dementia is getting worse. I thought I could handle this, but can I? What will she be like a month from now or in a year? Can I handle this situation until I'm eighteen and an adult? I'm starting to wonder.
Funny, I feel like writing a spell to take away her desire to make me think I'm a witch. How's that for weird?

***

"Hey, Mr. Journalist," growled Bear who was climbing up the ladder out of the now fifty-foot deep pit. "I think you need to get your nose out of your book and come look at this."

Jimmy and Tom helped Bear climb off the ladder, and once he was on solid ground again, he pulled a board out of his backpack. The board looked like a plaque, but instead of writing, the plaque had three deep gouges across it.

"Is this similar to what they found at the real Money Pit?" asked Tom. "Because we've hit the fifth platform down there. This was lying on top of it."

Sean picked up the plaque and examined it. "Not exactly. It was a stone tablet with writing on it. I don't know what to make of this thing."

"But still, this could be it, right?" asked Tom. "The last platform? We pull this up and—whoosh!—the water floods in?"

Rubbing his temples, Sean replied. "It's a distinct possibility." He looked at the plague once more and sighed. "Yeah...probably a really good possibility, in fact."

"So what do we do now?" asked Jimmy, his eyes darting wildly from boy to boy. "Look for wires? Booby traps?"

Sean grimaced. He wished he had a good answer for them. "Some articles have suggested that a booby trap mechanism wasn't needed, that the platforms themselves were the mechanism. You see, they act like a cork in a champagne bottle. The liquid inside is being contained under pressure and when you remove the pressure..."

"Pop!" said Jimmy enthusiastically. Then his face turned to a frown. "Oh..."

"So what do we do now?" asked Bear.

"Well, I have an idea," started Tom with a sly smile, reaching out and taking the plaque from Sean. He looked at it for a long moment, then added, "But first you guys have to promise you won't get mad."

"Oh, no way, no way! You didn't!" started Bear, his eyes practically glowing with rage. "You did *not* tell your dad!"

Tom nodded and smiled confidently as though he were proud of it. "I most certainly did."

"Damn it, Tom! We said no! More times than I can count, we said no!" shouted Sean.

"What else are we going to do?!" Tom shouted back, now venting his own frustration. His 'Mr. Perfect' façade had completely evaporated away, and all that remained was a very angry teenager. "We need engineers to figure this out and technology to see what's down there. We can't do this alone."

"Your dad is going to take it all and leave us nothing," growled Bear, standing next to Sean, facing off with Tom. "We're just a bunch of dumb kids to him. He'll give us a pat on the head and a tiny little finder's fee!"

"If even that," remarked Sean. "My guess is he'll just give us the pat on the head."

"My dad wouldn't do that!"

"Come on, guys, let's calm down," said Jimmy approaching the three. "Everything is going to be fine. You just need to calm down."

"You calm down! I'm tired of you guys always acting like my dad is a thief!" said Tom as he gave Jimmy a hard shove.

Jimmy tumbled backward and fell on top of a mound of dirt.

"What the hell's wrong with you!" yelled Sean, grabbing Tom by the collar with one hand and waving his fist in the other boy's face, inches from his nose. "Jimmy didn't do anything to you! What, you've been nice to him for a couple months so you think that gives you the right to beat him up again now? Because you what, took a break? The kind, gentle vegan, right? What a damn joke! You were a bully when you were a little kid, and you're a bully now!"

At this accusation, Tom's face turned pale and the fight in him seemed to drain away. "I didn't mean to do that. It just happened." He then turned to Jimmy and said, "I'm sorry. Gosh, man, I'm really sorry!"

Jimmy nodded, but Sean wasn't satisfied with this simple apology. He shoved Tom back, releasing his collar at the last second. This time it was Tom who stumbled and nearly fell to the ground. On regaining his footing, he shot an angry look at Sean, one that was dripping with venom. "Tom, I want you to get the hell out of here. Just freakin' leave!"

Tom's jaw dropped open, stunned. "What? You can't order me away! This is as much my treasure as it is yours."

"We're not ordering you away, Tom," said Bear, his anger having also vanished, replaced by something that looked akin to fear. The situation was spinning out of control, and their friendships were now on the line. "We just need a cooling off period. Right, Sean? Right?"

Sean and Tom were silently glaring at each other.

"Yeah. Sure. Whatever," growled Sean.

Tom finally backed up and began to walk toward the path, tucking the plaque under his arm. But then he slowed his pace. Abruptly, he whirled around, faced the other three boys and said, "You can order me away all you want, but my dad bought this ravine a couple days ago, so in the end, I'm still going to be part of this. Legally, my family owns the pit and everything in it now. It's you guys who need permission to be here. I'm willing to share, don't get me wrong, but you can't cut me out, so don't even try."

He then turned and stomped up the path with Jimmy, Bear and Sean staring after him in shock.

***

Sean laid in bed that night, staring up at the ceiling, thinking about the fight. Glancing toward his nightstand, he saw his journal and remembered the ridiculous curse he had placed on Tom that afternoon when he got home.

Very mature, Sean, very mature, he thought to himself.

The fight was all so stupid. He hadn't genuinely believed they would get down to the treasure and still didn't believe it. Either it was not a treasure pit, in which case there was no treasure, or it was designed like the Money Pit, and if that happened, no one could get down to the treasure. Either way, they'd never get anything, so why fight over it? Why get so angry at

The Hunted Tribe: Rocket's Red Glare

Tom?

Because he shoved Jimmy, that's why.

"Oh, yeah," he muttered to his empty bedroom.

They had to work it out, they had to. This was his home, and the guys were his friends. Somehow, someway he had to make things better. Certainly their friendships were more important than that stupid pit.

Tom's last words echoed in his memories, and he wondered if they would even be able to get back to the pit. Would his dad erect a fence around the pit now to keep out trespassers? Visions of the fence entered his thoughts along with images of armed security guards patrolling the area.

"Oh, man," grumbled Sean, shaking his head. "What kind of friend would do that to us? If we go down there and find a fence around it, that's it I swear…it's game over. Tom will have to find some new friends."

As he contemplated this, his eye lids grew heavy and he yawned loudly.

On an impulse, Sean turned his nightstand light on and looked at the pad of paper peeking out at him from under the desk. The line that read "You're almost out of time," had been crossed out and above it was a new line. "Time is up, Sean. I'm so very sorry."

"Son of a..," grumbled Sean, feeling his blood pressure spike. "I'm sick to death of you! You're going into the fireplace tomorrow, and I'm going to light you up like a roman candle."

Angrily, he switched off the light and closed his eyes, fuming at the whole situation. Whether he wrote the message or somehow his grandmother did it, he would find a way to make it stop.

Think of something else for now, Sean. Just…think of something else…

It took a moment to find a pleasant topic, but his mind finally settled on the day he arrived on the island. It had really been such a good day. He smiled as he thought about his birthday gifts and eating out at his favorite restaurant. Before long, his breathing grew more regular and relaxed, and he felt himself start to slip into the misty world of sleep once more.

His mind drifting more freely now, and he thought about his strange dreams those early days. They had been about a Dwanake tribesman who lived during the Civil War times and assumed the identity of an Indian from Calcutta, Srinam Srinivasan, to escape the Grishla.

I'm almost sorry that dream ended, he thought to himself as he began to fall into a deep slumber. The Grishla had found Srinam and his infant daughter in his last dream. *I wonder what happened? My grandmother said since he was my ancestor I have to stop him from dying too. Talk about a tall order. Still, I wondered what happened.*

To his surprise, he found himself back in the all too familiar surroundings…

***

Srinam ran down the gully, hearing only too clearly the heavy footprints of the creature behind him—and it was gaining on him fast.

Quickly he dodged into the bushes, thinking of a rabbit being pursued by a coyote. The rabbit's advantage was that he was small and more maneuverable in the thick bushes. Srinam could use this to his advantage as well.

He ducked into some bushes and heard the crash of the creature behind him; it was getting closer, so very much closer. Srinam realized too late his mistake. He was not a rabbit hiding from a coyote, he was a rabbit hiding from an enraged bull elephant who could simply crash through the trees and undergrowth to reach his prey.

Srinam leapt up with the intent of running toward

The Hunted Tribe: Rocket's Red Glare

the creek, but instead tripped over a rock. Thinking quickly, he turned to his side to protect Nina from the impact of the fall. He landed hard, his head momentarily hitting a rock. Baby Nina screamed at the top of her lungs while Srinim groaned and rubbed the growing lump on his head.

"Get up!" yelled Sean. "Get up!"

Srinam gasped and turned to look up at Sean. "Who are you? Where did you come from?"

For the very first time since Sean started having these dreams, he was now in the dream himself. *Oh, man, this isn't good,* thought Sean to himself.

"My name is Sean, I'm here to help you," he stammered, regretting the words instantly. How could he possibly help? But this was the truth, at least according to his grandmother.

He heard something large charging though the bushes and stop just a few feet away. A large figure now lurked in the shadows of a tall pine. Penetrating red eyes, towering nearly two feet above Sean's head, stared down at him from only a foot away at most.

Sean and Srinam were both too close to the creature to escape.

***

A night owl hooted, giving Tom a shiver of apprehension. It sure was spooky down in the ravine at this time of night.

"Hello!" called Tom, as he approached the pit. "Is anyone out here?"

He received no answer.

He shook his head and mumbled to himself. "After that bear attack, I really don't like to be out in the woods at night. This is a bad idea."

It didn't make sense to Tom. Sean called him and told him to come out to the pit. He insisted, wanted to talk to Tom alone, work things out without Bear and

Jimmy getting in the way.

He figured Sean was planning on decking him. Okay, he probably deserved it. He did lie to the group. So, Tom's plan was to let Sean get in one good punch. Just one. Then Tom would sit on top of him if he had to and make him listen to reason. This was the only way they were going to get to the treasure. Period. There was no reason for it to end their friendship.

As he waited for Sean to arrive, he examined his surroundings with the flash light. There was no movement, no noise.

Didn't the forest grow quiet when that bear showed up on our camping trip? It occurred to him. *I'm assuming it was in response to the presence of a large predator—but if that's the case, does that mean the quiet now could mean...*

More carefully, Tom flashed his light around the pit.

And then, he thought heard something. A slight movement and then another.

The sound was coming from the pit.

Tom thought his heart would stop when a mournful howl suddenly rose from the pit.

"Oh, no!" he said. "Everybody got so angry after the fight we left the pit open and some poor deer or something fell in!"

The cry came again, low and long. There was something disturbing about it, menacing. Yet, also familiar.

"The dog! That's the sound the wounded dog made that we followed it down here in the ravine."

He heard the soft whimper, the unmistakable cry of a dog, begging for help.

"Puppy, is that you?" called down Tom to the bottom of the pit.

A happy bark answered his reply.

"Oh, man, what have we done?" he said, grabbing the ladder and swinging his leg over to climb down it. "I'm coming! I'm coming!"

Climbing down the ladder was difficult with one hand, so he fumbled with the flashlight to put it in his pocket. Instead, it slipped from his wet fingers and tumbled into the pit with a loud clatter, striking the ladder a few times on the way down. Tom cringed, terrified it would hit the dog, but instead it landed on the wood planks below with a soft *thunk*. He groaned and examined the darkness below him. The flashlight briefly spun on the floor of the pit, occasionally catching a dark form. The dog was definitely down there.

"I'm coming, boy, it's okay," said Tom, working his way down.

He could see something moving in front of the flashlight, pacing. Waiting for him to reach the bottom. It acted impatient.

It has to be the dog, right? thought Tom again. *That was a dog bark earlier, right?*

An impossibly loud, mournful cry rose from the bottom of the pit once again, and he felt his blood turn to ice. The sound echoed in the tight quarters, the bone-chilling cry striking Tom from every angle. It took every ounce of courage he had to keep from scrambling out of that pit.

Is it the dog? his mind questioned. *You're sure it's the dog? You're absolutely certain?*

The soft bark came again, and Tom sighed. Dropping his head against his arm that was draped across one of the wooden rungs, he took a slight breather. Tom's wavy, blonde hair cascaded over the sleeve of his 'Rocket's Red Glare' brand denim jacket with the American flag patch on both sleeves. He stayed there a moment, allowing himself a chance to calm down.

"Please stop with that howl," called down Tom once he felt like he had the nerve to descend the ladder once more. "I don't think my heart can handle that again."

He continued down the ladder, focusing instead on

how he would get the dog out. First, he decided, to check him over to see if he was hurt. Then he would tie the rope around the dog, the one they had been using to lift up buckets of dirt, and hoist the animal out of the pit.

The light in the bottom of the pit no longer showed a pacing form. There was no movement. Tom sensed whatever was down there was waiting for him. Watching him.

Dog, thought Tom. *Not whatever is down there, the dog.*

"It's okay, boy, it's okay," said Tom in a soothing voice as he took the last two rungs of the ladder and finally stepped on the floor of the pit. "Are you hurt, are..."

That was when Tom smelled it. Not the smell of wet dog as he expected, but something else, something repulsive. It smelled familiar, yet the memory seemed to be just beyond his reach. Slowly it came back to him. This was how it smelled at the zoo in the snake house.

A sudden movement in front of the flashlight, a tail. Tom gasped as the shape and form of the tail registered in his mind. The tail was massive, a good five feet long, and it was covered in black and white feathers. The remarkable appendage undulated like a crocodile tail.

He couldn't imagine what it was…but either way, he knew it wasn't a dog.

Panic took hold, and Tom lunged for the ladder. With an ear-piercing scream—the same scream he had heard coming from the creature who had attacked them on that unforgettable night in June—something huge knocked him to the ground. Razor sharp teeth tore through his jacket and into his shoulder and with one sudden jerk, Tom felt his collar bone snap.

The pain was so sudden and beyond anything he could have ever imagined. Tom wailed in both terror and complete agony as the creature kept him pinned down in the mud under its incredible weight and continued to work at destroying what was left of his shoulder in sharp, jerking motions, eventually pulling his arm free from the socket. Tom's shrieked, punching the creature as hard as he could with his one free arm to no avail. And then, just as suddenly, the creature jumped off him and scampered up the ladder.

"Oh God! Oh God!" gasped Tom, feeling the blood gushing from around his now lifeless arm that laid limply in the mud, only barely attached to him by skin and bone.

I've got to get out of here, I've got to get out of here before that thing comes back! He told himself, wondering how he could possibly climb out of the pit and get help with his arm in its current condition.

Snap! Crack!

Tom heard a sound above him, and his entire body clenched. *Is it coming back? Is it coming back?* He wondered. *Please, please, don't let that be the thing coming back!*

Tom got his wish, but not in the way he would have wanted.

Crack! Crack!

Tom blinked and shook his head as muddy water drizzled down on top of him, seeping into his eyes and mouth. He choked and coughed and forced himself to sit up despite the pain, bewildered and alarmed. It took him a few shocked seconds to realize that the sides of the pit were beginning to break open.

"Oh! No! No!" cried out Tom, scrambling off the floor of the pit and staggering to the ladder. His legs felt like lead and his head began to spin, but he didn't allow himself to stop and think about any of that. He had seconds at most, and he knew it.

You've got to get out of here, Tom! Move! Move! He told himself. He pulled himself up one rung and then two, his uninjured arm taking on the work of two. *You can do this, man, come on, just do it!*

With a thunderous roar, the sides of the pit gave way all at once and tons of water, mud and rocks crashed in on Tom, knocking him back down to the floor of the pit and crushing him beneath their intense weight.

Chapter Eleven

In the darkness of the pines, Sean saw movement. Tree limbs swayed and the pine needles on the forest floor shifted and snapped as padded feet gently walked upon them. The motion was deliberate, stealthy—predatorial. He knew what it was, knew it could only be one thing, the very thing he had been hearing about for months now.

This was it; he would finally see the Grishla.

Despite all of his dreams, despite possibly even being chased through the forest by the creature, he had never once seen it. The problem was, dream or not, he didn't want to see it.

It's just a dream, Sean, he told himself as his fear began to mount. *It can't hurt you.* However, recalling how Srinam was now able to see him, he wondered if this was true. He was in the dream now, trapped in a face-to-face confrontation with the Grishla.

The tree limbs parted and the creature stepped into the light. Sean felt the blood drain from his face. It wasn't at all like he had expected or would have ever imagined. In fact, the creature didn't even look real. It had blue skin with bright aquamarine, green, and yellow feathers. The eyes he did recognize, however. Menacing, glowing red orbs, just like that night in the forest with the guys.

So, it really was the Grishla that had chased after us, he thought to himself. *How in the world did Jimmy ever mistake this for Bigfoot?*

As it stepped closer to them, its red eyes focused on him and Srinam, Sean felt weak in the knees. They were standing so close to it—much too close. He could make out the rhythmic breathing under the feathers, and as the creature's lips parted, revealing razor sharp teeth, Sean was able to even make out the serration on the front fangs.

Sean's mouth went dry, and he could barely breathe.

They couldn't run, it would leap on them and kill them instantly. They couldn't stay, the Grishla was there to kill them. *We have to do something! We have to! Think, Sean, think!* But he knew they were trapped.

"You should have made the choice, Srinam," came a voice from the Grishla, making Sean jump.

This was more unexpected than the technicolor feathers. Even more confusing, the voice did not come from its mouth. Sean wasn't quite sure what had just happened.

"If you had chosen to sacrifice yourself, committed suicide, I would have spared the child. Now, both of you shall die."

Sean was stunned. What did it say? It would have spared Nina if Srinam had committed suicide? Why would it say that? Why would it even care about that? More than that, Sean was astounded by where the voice had come from. The voice was coming from a small metal box strapped around the creature's neck by a leather strap.

Why would a spirit guide need to use some kind of device to talk through? Even if this is a dream, this doesn't make any sense.

"No, please!" begged Srinam, who then turned to Sean. "Please, Sean, help me fight this terrible beast and save my child!"

The Grishla's head whipped toward Sean, and he felt his heart stop. But it did not seem to see him and continued to pivot its head from one direction to another.

Sean felt something inside of him snap. *What if his grandmother was telling him the truth? What if it was his destiny to face the Grishla?*

At that moment he decided it was true—always had been true. He was born for this one purpose. The Grishla was not a lie; instead, his dreams of a normal future were the lie. This was it. This was where he would either defeat the Grishla or it would defeat him.

The war had final begun.

"Run!!" yelled Sean as he launched himself toward the creature.

Srinam did as he was told, grabbed his baby, and jumped to his feet.

However, things did not work out as Sean had planned and only a half a second later, he realized that he had made a terrible mistake.

Instead of hitting the Grishla in the side, he passed straight through the it as if Sean was merely a ghost. The Grishla was not thrown off his feet the way he had anticipated, leaving the creature free to react to Srinam's movement. It leapt upon the running man with a ferocious screech, knocking him to the ground. Baby Nina, in wails of panic, flew from his arms and landed hard on the dirt path. As Sean helplessly watched, the creature reached down with his muzzle, latched onto Srinam's head with its ferocious teeth, and with a single, violent jerk and a loud snap, Srinam's entire body spasmed, then fell still.

With a casual air, the Grishla dropped Srinam from his jaws, the limp body falling to the ground with an empty thud. Srinam's blank, staring eyes looked up at Sean, the dead man's head twisted at an unnatural angle and a single tear rolling down his cheek. All life within the man was gone, all in a single instant. His eyes seemed to say, "You did this to me, Sean. You said you were here to save us and I trusted you."

Swallowing hard, Sean stumbled back, his own

failure feeling like a punch to the stomach. *This isn't what was supposed to happen...*

The creature then stepped forward, and in slinky, almost elegant movements it walked toward the crying baby.

"No, not the baby, please not her!" cried Sean.

The Grishla leaned down toward baby Nina, its snake-like head tilting one direction and then the next as it curiously examined the helpless child.

"NO!!" screamed Sean, suddenly sitting up in his bed.

The dream was over, done. Sean shook violently knowing with complete certainty that this had not been a dream. He was responsible for Srinam's death. For several long seconds, he sat there, barely able to contain the grief and guilt.

"No, it's not true. it was a dream; it was a dream!" it tried to tell himself. "It has to be; it can't be real! None of this is real!"

Sean thought about the day, the fight with Tom, and told himself he was just reacting to the argument. His eyes glanced over toward the desk. Peering into the inky darkness, he wondered if the message on the pad had changed once more. It had said it was already too late…too late…

The pad of paper is right, Sean, came the voice of Hugo the Jerk. Over the past few weeks, Hugo's voice had changed, grown deeper, more course and toxic. *It's all too late, all because you didn't listen to your grandmother everyone is going to die...*

Stop it, stop it, stop! His words twisting into a desperate whimper. *You're not real, go away, go away!*

Ha, ha, ha, ha, ha, hee, hee, hee, HEE, HEE, hee, hee...

Laughter...first a mocking laugh, then it grew strange and maniacal.

Overwhelmed, Sean grabbed his hair with both hands and suppressed a scream.

"Go away, just go away!"

There's only one way to end it, Sean, you know it and I know it. Go to your grandmother's room...

Hugo, stop it! Cried Richard the Sensible, suddenly breaking into the conversation.

Sean pulled his knees up to his chin and he rocked back and forth, his very sanity cracking at the edges.

Go into her closet...

No! shrieked Richard, now in near hysterics. *No! Sean, don't do it!*

Pull out her rifle and put the muzzle under your chin...

"*GO AWAY!! GO AWAY!!!*"

"*Sean!*" came his grandmother's voice, breaking the spell.

With an embarrassed yelp, Sean looked up. "Grandma!"

She rushed over to him from the door way, grabbed his shoulders, and stared deeply into his eyes. Her hair was sticking out in all directions and the panic in her voice rang clear as a bell. "Is it the Grishla? Did you have a vision of him? Has he started killing people again?"

"Ugh," grumbled Sean in frustration. Not this again, not now. "No...nothing like that grandma, just a nightmare."

"Srinam?" she asked, her voice cracking on the mere mention of the name.

Internally, Sean groaned. *Enough already*, he thought. "No, no Grishla, and no Srinam. It was a normal nightmare. Um...werewolves. I was being chased by werewolves." *A joke, Sean, turn it into a joke. It will change the mood, calm her down. Maybe calm me down too.* "They...they wanted to dress me in a pink, satin, evening gown for the werewolf ball..."

His made-up dream had the desired effect, she let out a soft chuckle and shook her head. "Well, I think it's safe for me to say that was not a premonition."

"I don't know, grandma, I look pretty darn cute in pink," he said, batting his eyelashes in a feminine fashion. *Please laugh again,* his mind pleaded. *I need to hear something pleasant like laughter and know there is more to life than this nightmare I'm living...*

As though ordered to do so, his grandmother laughed loudly. "Well, those werewolves will just have to catch you and put you in that pink gown to prove it me. For now, what do you say we get up and get some breakfast?"

"Breakfast?" asked Sean forcing a laugh into his own voice. "It's the middle of the night."

"Breakfast might be a few hours early, but something tells me neither of us are going to get back to sleep now. Might as well have a nice long breakfast, relax and ease our way into the day. How do waffles and your favorite coffee sound?"

Sean practically choked at the words. "Are you kidding? After all of the diet food you've had me eating…you don't even have to ask, I'm there!"

She smiled, got to her feet and started to ruffle his no doubt already ruffled hair, but then suddenly stopped and pulled back her hand. With a frown she examined her fingers then looked at him. "You might want to take a shower before you come down," she said, then reaching down and tugging on the damp sheets that stuck to his sweat-slick skin. "And there are fresh sheets down the hall, in the linen cupboard. Take your time, I'll have your breakfast ready when you come down."

With that, she turned and left the room, closing the door behind her.

"Oh, gosh…ick!" said Sean pulling back the sheets away from his soaked through pajamas. He was completely drenched in sweat. At least…he hoped it was just sweat.

Hearing his grandmother's footsteps leading away from his room, he then quietly whispered, "Hugo? Are you still there? Richard?"

In the distance, crickets sang back and forth to each other, but Hugo and Richard were both notably—and mercifully—absent.

"It was exactly what you told your grandmother," said Sean. "Except the part about the werewolves. It was a nightmare, nothing more. Everything will be better tomorrow, I swear. Tomorrow will be fantastic. We'll make up with Tom, we'll find the treasure, and everything is going to be fine. I know it is."

Sean looked at his clock: 4:12 am; it was later than he thought. The sun would be rising soon. Tomorrow was now today.

For some unknown reason, this filled him with dread. Some part of him told him that this was the day, the very day he had been waiting for, yet dreading, his entire life.

Stop it, Sean, stop! You've got to get a grip. Today is a normal day like any other.

***

Back in New York, in the darkness of Sean's empty bedroom which he had not seen since late May, a spark flickered on his old bedspread. The flicker quickly erupted into flame and within seconds, the blue flame spread across the bed. The room began to fill with smoke and a high-pitched smoke alarm screamed into the night.

Chapter Twelve

Jimmy waited impatiently as the phone rang. He looked outside at the rising sun and twisted his fingers around the phone cord.

Today was going to be a big day.

"Hello?" a woman's voice answered.

"Aunt Becky, it's me, Jimmy," he said excitedly.

"Jimmy!" Her voice was elated. "You timed it perfectly, we just arrived at the farm house. The kids are thrilled. They're looking forward to autumn here in New England."

Jimmy laughed. "It's quite a bit like the autumn here on the island, but don't tell them that. Still, you're at a maple farm, so the trees should be spectacular."

Becky laughed. "It *is* beautiful! I can't believe you got me this job at the museum, working on the lost Roanoke colony site! I told them I didn't have any archeological experience, but it was like you said, they didn't care. They just need someone to log the files and the other finds. And it pays so much better than my last job."

Jimmy smiled broadly, feeling a thrill rush through him on hearing how pleased she was.

"It's so strange the way they found the lost members of the Roanoke colony way up here in Maine," she said, a haunting tinge to her words. "And...the last people who worked at the site died too I found out. They were killed by some large animal...just like the

Roanoke colony members. I guess I can see why no one else wanted the job…"

Jimmy tensed. *Darn it, why did she have to hear about that? I wanted her to feel safe and happy.*

"Aunt Becky, I swear, it's perfectly safe," insisted Jimmy. "Lots of people have worked at the site since then and now they have electric fences around it to protect the grounds."

There was a pause.

"Yes…um…I saw that. This place has the security of Fort Knox." Aunt Becky cleared her throat and said, "But it doesn't matter. The farm is beautiful! And you just knew some elderly woman who pulled some strings? Who is this woman? Why did she go to so much effort for you?"

"Oh, I paid her back in watching many hours of Doris Day films, believe me," said Jimmy, with a laugh." His voice grew serious and he added. "The truth is, Aunt Becky, I told her about my situation, about how I wanted to change my life. She's on the board of directors, can you believe it?"

Jimmy, paused wondering if he should tell her more, tell her that the woman had left him her shares in the company when she passed away in June and the truth was, as a major stockholder in the company, *he* had arranged for Aunt Becky to live on the farm. Jimmy was now officially filthy rich and owned the farm house, lock, stock and barrel. *It's too much,* thought Jimmy. *I'll be with them soon and the truth about everything will come out by then anyway.*

"Jimmy, are you still there?"

He coughed, and said, "Yes, yes. I was just thinking. We're going to have a great life, Aunt Becky." He pumped up the enthusiasm in his voice. This was a time of joy and celebration, he needed her to hear it in his voice. "You, me and the kids. We're all going to have a productive, worry-free life from now on. The kids aren't going to end up like Mom and Dad; they're not going to throw away their lives drinking themselves into oblivion."

"What about you, Jimmy?" asked Aunt Becky, her voice stern. "How is your drinking problem?"

Jimmy froze, horrified.

"Dennis…he told you didn't he?" he said quietly. He felt sick.

"Yes he did," she said. "He said last summer, you started drinking. He said you started checking out like your parents, lost your job at the grocery store and even… He even said one night…"

As Aunt Becky paused, he cringed. He didn't want to hear this. *Why did she have to find out about all that? Why?*

"He said you hit him."

Jimmy felt his hands begin to shake. "I was tired, and he was yelling at me, telling me I was just like mom and dad and…I snapped…I just…" he shook his head hard. "No, look forget all of what I just said. I was wrong. There's nothing I can say to make what happened right. Ever. But I can tell you I've changed. I spent the last few months completely dry. That's why I sent them to you, I needed the time to get clean and it worked. I'm not that person anymore. I wish I could think of a way to convince you…"

"I wouldn't have taken this new job if I wasn't already convinced of that."

Jimmy paused and blinked hard; he hadn't anticipated that response.

"After he told me what happened, I've been checking up on you. You got a new job at Judy's Hardware store. You've been mowing lawns and even helping the elderly. In the last few months you have been a changed boy. Jimmy, I'm so proud of you!"

Jimmy swallowed hard. "I'm determined to make a new life for myself, Aunt Becky. If nothing else, please believe that. I plan to go to school in Maine, work for the museum, help take care of the kids. I'm going to give them a better life. I'm going to give *all of us* a better life. We're escaping this nightmare, once and for all."

"Good for you, honey," said Aunt Becky. "But why are you still waiting to come up to join us?"

"I've been working on a project with some buddies of mine, and I have to see it through to the end. It looks like we're close to the end." He was careful not to say treasure pit, he didn't want to sound like a lunatic. "And then I'll come up, I promise."

"Just get up her when you can," she said. "I know you want to stay behind and care for your parents…"

"No, no, my dad got his money in early," lied Jimmy. "He can afford to have that maid take care of the house. They don't need me anymore…they never needed any of us, really."

"Nor do you need them," remarked Aunt Becky. "I've filed the custody papers for you and the kids. You're free now. No more."

Jimmy nodded, once again forgetting she couldn't see him. "I'll see you soon. I love you. Tell the little ones I love them too. I'd ask to talk to them but we both know they won't talk to me…"

"Once you're up here, it will be easier to mend fences," she replied in a consoling voice. "Good bye. I love you too."

As the phone clicked, Jimmy picked up his packed duffle bag off the kitchen counter and walked into the living room. He clicked off the television and turned to look at his parents. They stared back at him with emotionless eyes.

"That's it, I'm done here," he said looking from one to the other. "You're on your own now."

Their stare did not falter nor did either of them say a word. He hadn't really expected them too, but this was the end of his old life and the beginning of his new one. Somehow, it felt like someone should say more.

"I'm going to do for those kids what you wouldn't,"

said Jimmy. "They're going to have a good life. They're going to go to college and they're going to be happy. You two threw away your lives, and so did the old Jimmy. If it makes you feel any better, I almost hate the old Jimmy more than you. He was all those kids had, he was their only hope and then he turned to alcohol like you and completely abandoned them..." A half sob caught in Jimmy's throat, and he looked down at his hands. They were clenched into tight fists and were shaking violently. *This is why you became a Christian, remember?* He told himself. *To get away from your angry past, let it go...just let it go...time to start a new life.* Clearing his throat, Jimmy said, "I'm tired of this game of pretend. It ends here. No more. I'm done here."

Jimmy turned to the door and paused, then took a step back and clicked on the television set.

"Actually, I want to remember you guys like this," he said with a half growl. "Alone with your two loves: alcohol and the TV!"

Finally, he opened the front door, stepped out onto the porch, closed the door behind him and took in a deep breath.

What a glorious morning! he thought to himself. *What an amazing, wonderful day! You can almost smell the promise of hope in the air.*

For a second he paused, thinking about the kids in Maine, excited about autumn. Halloween would be coming soon, and he could take the kids trick-or-treating—their first one ever, thanks to their freak of a mom. He knew, though, it would never be as wonderful of a night as the made up Halloween night that Tom and the guys had created for him. He patted his bag, glad he'd packed his Zorro costume. He never wanted to forget that night.

With a playful laugh, he jumped off the porch and yelled "It is time for the pirates of the Elk Island Money Pit to face El Zorro, master of the blade and hero of the people! Today I shall take back our birth right and free my people!"

He laughed, heading to the clubhouse to drop off his bag. After that, straight to Sean's house.

Chapter Thirteen

Long black hair draped over Sean's face, hiding the tears running down his cheeks. One trembling hand wiped away the tears while the other hand held his cell phone to his ear. Sean paced the floor of his bedroom, listening to his father's endless rant.

"But I didn't do it. I'm here!" protested Sean once again.

At the other end of the line, his father continued to scream at him without pause or hesitation. He wasn't listening to Sean; he probably hadn't heard a single word.

"No more staying at your Grandmother's house! You're coming back to New York. We've located a reform school, and we've already registered you. No more of this, Sean! No more!"

The bedroom door slammed open, hitting the wall with a bang. His grandmother charged into the room, her face angry and tight. Sean took a stumbling step back. He had never seen her this angry before. Despite her age, she looked like a warrior about to enter battle.

"I just had it out with your mother on the phone downstairs. Let me talk to your father. It's his turn!"

Sean nodded and gratefully handed her his cell.

"You listen to me right...Henry, will you please hush up? Henry!"

Sean rubbed his eyes again, trying to fight back the tears. He was sixteen, far too old to cry, but it was all so frustrating! The old man never listened! Guilty until proven innocent. Nothing ever changed.

Reform school! His worst nightmare had been realized.

"Henry, you can't possibly blame Sean for this! Yes, I've been with him the entire time. Now why would I leave the island for a couple days? He didn't do it, and you know it... I don't care where the fire started, he's... Now why would he start a fire on his own bed, that's ridiculous!"

His grandmother looked over at him and, in an exaggerated gesture, rolled her eyes to the ceiling. Sean returned a weak smile. His grandmother always sided with him. He should have never doubted that.

"Henry...Henry, listen to me! Sean and I are both still on Elk Island and we have never left. Do you remember where it is? You bought Sean's plane ticket, so you should! It's one of the San Juan islands off of the West Coast—the West Coast!—of Canada. *You* are in New York, all the way on the *East* Coast. There is an entire continent between us! How in the world would a sixteen-year-old boy...no, I'm sure he didn't get one of his friends to do it. I don't think he has any—"

His grandmother paused and her face froze. Guiltily, she glanced at Sean. He knew what she was going to say. She didn't think he had any friends in New York. And she was right. Despite living in New York the majority of his life, he had no one and nothing back there, just empty memories of misery. And in just two weeks he'd have to return. A wave of panic and nausea passed through him at the thought.

"Listen, Sean is doing very well here, you leave him alone," she said. "He's helping me with projects around the house and he's making friends with the local boys. They're good boys. In fact, one of them left a gift for Sean on the porch today."

Sean shot her a questioning glance and she nodded.

"I brought it in and left it for you on entryway table. Go down and open it."

She didn't have to tell him twice. He'd take any excuse to get out of that room and away from his father's accusations. Sean turned and bolted for the door.

"Wait. Sean, wait." He skidded to a stop.

Oh, no! Now what?

"Henry, I'm calling you back on the house phone. Make sure your wife doesn't pick up, I'm not speaking with her."

She hung up the cell phone and handed it back to Sean. "I'm going into my bedroom and talk to your father. Go downstairs and open your present. I don't want you picking up the language I'm planning on using, you hear?"

Sean nodded, grabbed the cell phone and darted out of the room without looking back. He ran down the stairs at top speed, his feet striking the risers with such force and speed that it sounded like rapid gun fire. He had forgotten what his life had been like back home, all the anger and yelling. And now, with a single phone call, all that ugliness, all the poison from that terrible place hit him full force. Clear across the country and he was still being accused of things! How could he ever stand to return to New York? On hitting the landing, he continued his flight through the living room. He stopped to grab his backpack off of the couch and then turned toward the front door. He managed two determined steps forward before he stopped, frozen in place.

Sean remained motionless for a long moment, thinking. Abruptly he turned back to the couch, dropped the backpack, and began rummaging through the contents. His hand stopped. He found it! He extracted his Dark Journal and a pen. A smile crossed his face and he dropped into a chair next to the couch. The smile grew broader as he leafed through the journal. Finally, he reached an empty page and began to write.

The words were a carefully formed incantation, a curse, bringing suffering and misery upon his father, his mother, and sister. Sean paused, thought a moment, and crossed out the name of his sister. He and Stephanie had hated each other for a long time, but a few months ago they became allies in their war against Mom and Dad. No, he didn't have a problem with her anymore. She was almost a friend now.

Sean sat back in the chair, and stared into a mirror hanging above the fireplace. He sure looked different from when he first arrived. He'd lost a lot of weight. His once tight jacket was much looser now, except around his shoulders where he had built up considerable muscle tone from all of the digging. And despite the cool weather on the island, he sported a tan from all the hours spent working outside. That, combined with his long black hair, made him look like a true Native American now. What a change! Goodbye Pillsbury Dough boy, hello Native American warrior. Awesome!

Despite all of the craziness, his life had improved tremendously. He had friends, he had a home where people loved him. Now what was he returning to? Reform School and parents that treated him like a criminal? What was going to happen to him? What did he have to look forward to? How could he face that life? The tears began to come again, and he tried to force his mind to focus on something else. And that was when his eyes caught the color red in the mirror. Sean leaned forward to get a better look and saw a large present wrapped in red with a black bow sitting on top of the entryway table.

The present! He had completely forgotten about it! Sean leaped up, grabbed his backpack and ran into the entryway. He paused, staring at the gift, savoring the moment. The wrapping was too cool, deep red and

The Hunted Tribe: Rocket's Red Glare

black. Who sent it to him, though? And why? He ripped the wrapping and then stopped. The package contained a wooden plaque with odd symbols carved along all four sides. In the center of the plaque were three long scratches gouged deep into the wood. Sean stared at it for a long moment, wondering what it meant. Tom had taken this home with him last night. Why did he leave it for Sean all wrapped up like a present? A card dropped out of the wrapping, and Sean picked it up. It had one sentence written on it in red ink. "The task has been completed."

What did that mean? Was it Tom's way of saying he was quitting? A chill ran up his spine as another thought crossed his mind. The note said the *task* had been completed. And they had been working on only one task.

"Oh, no! No!" he yelled. "Damn it, Tom, it was just an argument! You didn't have to do this! You've ruined everything! Everything!"

He heard the bedroom door upstairs close. Sean shoved the wooden plaque into his backpack, swung it over his shoulder, and ran out the front door. The last thing he wanted to do was talk about the phone call, and he certainly didn't want to explain the plaque. He needed to get out there.

Sean jumped off the front porch and ran across the lawn, directly toward the trees. The woods were only a few hundred yards away. He'd be free and clear if he could make it to the tree line.

"Hey! I was coming to see you!" said a voice on his left. "Where are you going?"

Sean saw Jimmy running toward him.

"Come on!" He yelled.

"What?"

"Run to the trees! We need to get out of here. My grandmother's going to be looking for me any second!"

"Oh, okay," said Jimmy, quickly falling in line with

Sean.

That's Jimmy, he thought. *No questions. Simply goes along with everything. Easy going until the end. The complete opposite of Tom who liked to argue over everything.*

The two ran hard until they reached the trees. With the house out of sight, Sean stumbled to a stop, and Jimmy skidded to a halt beside him. The two stood in the shadows of the towering pines, an ominous silence enveloping them. Sean gulped in air as Jimmy stood patiently waiting for him to recover. It galled Sean that Jimmy wasn't even breathing hard. *Damn country kids!*

"So what's up?" asked Jimmy. "I thought you liked your grandmother."

"I do...I just want to avoid her....for right now."

"Okay." As usual, a simple acknowledgement, no prying questions.

Jimmy fell silent for a moment, but Sean knew this wouldn't last. It never did around Jimmy.

Sean sighed again. "We have a problem. I think Tom was a little angrier yesterday than I realized."

Sean pulled the plaque out of his backpack and handed it to Jimmy. An expression of confusion crossed Jimmy's face.

"He left it on my front porch all wrapped up like a gift along with a note saying 'The task has been completed.' I think it's his way of telling us that he's pulled up the last platform and triggered the bobby trap to flood the pit."

"What? Why would he do that?!"

"Why do you think? Because of that argument we got into yesterday."

Jimmy's face turned red and he started breathing harder.

"Chill, Jimmy, we'll work it out."

"We've worked for weeks on that damn pit! No, months! This is the most exciting thing that's ever happened on this stupid island. It was our own personal archeological dig; a pirate's treasure no less! And now it's all been ruined, ruined!"

"What's done is done—"

"No, I...I have to see," blurted out Jimmy, handing the plaque back to Sean. "I have to know."

Jimmy bolted down the path, toward the gully.

"Wait!" Sean called after him, roughly stuffing the plaque back into his backpack as he chased after his friend.

Chapter Fourteen

"Jimmy! Wait!" Sean called again.

Down the path, past the huge blackberry bushes, and through the small stand of birch trees he followed, falling farther and farther behind. Jimmy was too fast; he'd never catch up. Finally, exhausted, with a sharp pain throbbing in his side, Sean reached the top of the ravine. On a stretch of path several yards below him, he saw Jimmy running full speed into the deep ravine. Panting and light-headed, Sean slowed down to a walk. He watched as his friend rounded a hard dogleg in the path, disappearing from view. There was no hurry really; Sean knew where his friend was going.

Deep in thought, Sean made his way down the path, descending lower and lower into the ravine. A few patches of sunlight illuminated his way. The ravine was deep and dark with tall, old growth pines blocking out most of the sky. A chill hung heavily in the air even on the warmest day. And the disturbing silence. Not once had he ever seen a single bird or animal down here.

He thought about the day he first explored the gully. He was telling the guys the story of the Money Pit on Oak Island when they stumbled across the same scene off a hidden trail at the bottom of the gully. What were the odds? It still blew him away.

Sean was abruptly pulled out of his thoughts as he noticed that the patches of light on the ground were changing. The bright yellow light was turning red at the edges. Was he imagining it? He closed his eyes, opened them again, and saw the red color remained. Now the red seemed to be seeping into the yellow. The red swirled and expanded, choking out the natural sunlight. Sean looked up. The sky had turned red, expanding from one side of the tree-ragged opening to the other. A deep red. A blood red.

It couldn't be sunset! It was noon when he left the house! Sean stared up at the sky, stunned. Soon the red began to change. Black, menacing clouds began to emerge, converging to blot out the blood-red sky. The darkness was almost complete. Panic began to rise up into his throat. He could barely see. How would he ever find the pit, let alone his way out?! And what in the world would have caused the sky to turn that color?! Soon his eyes began to adjust, and he felt a few light sprinkles.

BOOM!

Thunder...there was a storm coming in off the ocean. In spite of himself, he breathed a sigh of relief. Just a storm. A completely normal storm. Somehow he felt like it was something more...something sinister...

Crack.

Sean's muscles tightened. Somewhere, below him in the darkness of the gully, something was moving. Perhaps Jimmy was coming back for him? Yet for some reason he didn't dare call out. It had to be Jimmy, who else would be down here? Still, he remained silent and still. A minute passed, then two. Had he really heard anything?

Snap. Crack. Crack.

Sean took a step back in silent alarm. No doubt about it this time. Something was moving below him, somewhere on the path. His eyes strained to see through the darkness, but there were only trees and an impenetrable wall of black. And then the sound changed. The unidentified thing suddenly picked up speed and charged toward the curve that lead up to him. But still he couldn't see anything.

Thinking back to their camping trip when the strange creature attacked them, Sean immediately began to panic.

What do I do? What do I do? Should I run? Should I hide? His mind raced through the options, knowing only too well he didn't have time for either.

Something huge, massive, reached the curve, and exploded out of the trees in front of him. A sharp object hit him hard in the forehead and he yelped, turning away. More things hit him, again and again. Sharp things, tiny things. Rocks? Twigs? Too late, he held up his backpack as a shield. His eyes stung and he blinked hard. And then it all faded away to a whimper. Quiet. It had been nothing more than the wind. A dust devil, perhaps? Sean looked down. Pine needles and dirt swirled around his feet through yellow patches of sun.

Yellow?

He refocused skyward. There were still a few black thunder bumpers up there, but they were now floating in a sea of blue sky.

"Geez!" gasped Sean. His grandmother had warned him that sometimes storms came in fast and hard, the perils of living on an island. And that's all it was. Nothing unusual at all.

Except that blood-red sky...

Sean began to run down the path. He didn't have that much farther to go, and while he would never admit it to anyone, he dreaded the idea of being alone in this dark, creepy forest a moment longer.

On reaching the bottom of the ravine, he took a small trail obscured by low-hanging trees. The path followed the creek for several yards, then took a sharp left. The ravine opened up into a small pocket of flat ground that no one else seemed to know existed. With the thick growth of trees, blackberry bushes, and ferns,

Sean wasn't surprised that this area had remained hidden for probably over a hundred years. He wondered how the pirates had found it. That is, if pirates had indeed created the pit. At this point, the guys still had no way of telling who created it.

As he cleared the trees, Sean found both Jimmy and Bear standing over the pit. They were staring intently down into it, a look of anger and frustration burned into their faces. Just as he had feared, the pit was flooded.

"Jimmy told me what Tom did," said Bear in his husky voice. "Not cool, man."

"Not cool," repeated back Jimmy, shaking his head.

"I think a storm is coming," said Sean. He paused. He didn't want to go home, but he didn't want to stay here any longer either. For some reason, the place was creeping him out more than usual today. Finally, he added, "Let's go back to the clubhouse and try to come up with a plan."

"It's the Northwest," grumbled Bear. "It rains here. Learn to deal."

"Yeah, just got to learn to deal," sighed Jimmy, nodding his head.

"Well, there isn't really anything we can do out here. We can't dig anymore."

"We can see where the water is coming from," said Jimmy, lifting a jar filled with a red liquid out of his pack.

Bear gruffly took the jar from him. He grunted as he held the jar up in the light. "What the hell is this?"

"Red dye," said Jimmy. "When the Money Pit on Oak Island flooded, they poured dye down the pit. I read about it at the library the other day. The dye seeped out and showed them where the water was coming in."

"And exactly how did you happen to bring this today?" asked Bear.

Jimmy shrugged. "I figured we'd have to pull up the

last platform eventually. So I made this up in my garage before I left."

There was an awkward silence.

Jimmy rolled his eyes. "I didn't pull up the platform, okay? I was just bringing this in case we decided to go that route."

"Fine," said Bear. "We believe you. So let's move on. The dye will help us figure out where the water is coming in, so we can figure out how to block the flow of water. But that didn't help them at the Money Pit."

"Well, no, it didn't," answered Jimmy. "Turned out the pirates had built multiple tunnels feeding water into the pit. The pirates even went so far as manufacturing an artificial beach filled with palm fronds to act as a filter to let the water in, but to keep the sand from blocking the channels. That's actually how they knew it wasn't the Native Americans, because there were no palm trees in that area. The people who built it had to have a ship. Totally cool!"

Bear sighed and rubbed a spot above his eye. He looked like he had a headache. "I know, man. Sean told us all this the other day."

"Exactly!" exclaimed Jimmy.

Sean and Bear exchanged glances. *Exactly what?*

Jimmy looked between the two of them, growing frustrated with their lack of enthusiasm. "Don't you see? Pouring the dye down the pit could give us vital clues as to who built this."

"Other than that," commented Bear. "What will it get us? Even when they found where the water was coming in, they still couldn't cut off the water completely."

"That's because the pit was pulling in water directly from the ocean from different sides of the island. Look around here. We're not that close to the beach and we're down in a rocky ravine. It's probably being fed by that creek. If that's the case, it only has one or two inlets. We should at least have a fighting chance of blocking it, don't you think?"

Sean and Bear nodded in agreement. There wasn't any flaw in his logic.

"Go for it," said Bear finally, handing him back the jar.

Jimmy quickly unscrewed the jar's lid and dumped the contents into the pit.

"Sorry, fish," said Sean toward the creek.

"So now what?" asked Bear. "Should we wander along the creek to see where the dye comes out?"

"I guess so," said Sean.

"Let's give it a couple minutes to filter through," said Jimmy. "This is going to be great! What if this whole ground we're standing on is riddled with palm fronds and some elaborate filtering system? I think that part is way cooler than some stupid treasure. This is an engineering miracle created by people hundreds and hundreds of years ago, like the pyramids, man!"

I doubt it was built "hundreds and hundreds of years back," thought Sean. He also wondered if this would really tell them anything about the builders. *Oh, well, Jimmy seems to be having fun.*

The wind whipped up again, and Sean pulled his coat tightly around his body. Summer was coming to a rapid end, all right. So early in the year, too. *Perhaps this is typical for the Northwest; this place seemed to run on the cold side on most days anyway.*

"Hand me the plaque again for a second," said Bear.

Sean handed it over and Bear examined it.

"I don't get those scratches in the middle," said Sean. "What could it mean?"

Bear put his hand over the three scratch marks, stretching his fingers out to match their position. The spread was wide on that end and Bear had some difficulty getting them to line up. Then he followed the scratches down the board, his hand following the lines as they went. Sean and Jimmy watched as Bear's hand went from being open wide to being pulled into a near fist.

"See how it goes wide and then draws in?" commented Bear. "It's like someone clawed this with their hand."

The Grishla? Thought Sean.

The conclusion was unavoidable.

Chapter Fifteen

It's that stupid dream of yours last night, Sean. It spooked you. Now calm down. The Grishla did not make this! Now get your brain on straight and think logically here.

"If it is from someone's hand, they were missing two fingers. Not to mention the vicious claws," said Jimmy. He then pointed to the middle mark, which was significantly wider and deeper. "The middle claw is bigger than the other claws."

Sean ran his fingers inside the channels in the wood. *Think logical, he told himself. What could it realistically be?* But despite his best efforts, it still looked like there was only one real solution. "Could be claw marks. Whatever made this, the ends of the fingers or tips of the instrument came to a sharp point. See how it's very narrow at the bottom of the channels and widens out?"

The three stood and stared at the plank of wood in silent contemplation for a long moment.

"An animal?" said Bear. "But what kind of animal would make a mark like this? And why put it at the bottom of a pit?"

"Weird," stated Jimmy. "Maybe it's a threat. I bet that's it."

Sean shrugged, but he was starting to feel nervous. *A threat from the Grishla is what my grandmother would say. No...just no. Cut it out, you're spooking yourself again.*

Sean felt his cell vibrating in his jacket pocket. He fished it out and looked at the caller ID. Stephanie! Why would his sister call him? She had never called him before. But then, maybe it wasn't her. Dad could have borrowed her phone, knowing Sean wouldn't pick it up if he saw his number. For a few brief moments, Sean considered his options. Finally, curiosity won out and he answered it. "Hello?"

"You are such a moron," his sister exclaimed into the phone. "If you pay me $100...no, $200...I'll keep your dirty little secret."

"What are you talking about, doofus?" asked Sean, annoyed.

"You *are* here! Or you hired someone to sneak into the house or something," said Stephanie. "But leaving one of your freaky little curses on my pillow, why would you do that? I thought you and I were doing okay lately. Fine, if that's the way you want it, war, it is!"

Sean scratched his head, baffled. "What? You found one of my old curse pages?"

"I don't know if it is old or not," she said. "I appreciate that you crossed my name off of it, though. At least that's some improvement."

Sean felt his breath stop. He had always included her on the curses and had never crossed her name of the list...until today...

"Wait a sec," he yelled into the phone.

"What?"

He dropped the phone to the ground, opened his backpack and dug through it. He pulled out his journal and frantically leafed through the pages. In his haste, he dropped the book awkwardly to the ground with a thud. The journal plopped open to his last entry...or what would have been his last entry. The page was gone, roughly torn out of the book. Jagged edges of paper remained behind.

The Hunted Tribe: Rocket's Red Glare

Sean stared down at it shocked. He wrote this entry about an hour ago at most. And the backpack had been on his shoulder the entire time. And even if it had left his sight, how could the pages possibly make their way to the house in New York, some three thousand miles away? He wracked his brain trying to think of another time where he crossed out her name, but nothing came to mind. And who would have put it on her pillow anyway?

"Sean, dude, you okay?" asked Bear.

Bear and Jimmy were staring at Sean, the drama with the pit momentarily forgotten.

"Yeah, you seem kind of freaked," added in Jimmy.

"Sean! Sean!" his sister's shouting came from his cell.

Sean grabbed the phone and picked it up.

"Stephanie..," his voice trailed off into silence. He didn't know what to say.

"I'm really more interested in your latest trick," she continued. "How did you get that red dye in the pipes? Man, you should have seen the look on Dad's face when he saw it! You better never come home. He's ready to cream you!"

"Red dye?" He gasped.

Stephanie laughed. "Yeah, pretty cool. Blood-red dye is coming out of every faucet!" There was a pause. "Dad just left. He's going to the hardware store for something. Wonder how he's going to fix this? Oh well, his problem. So how did you do it? Come on, you owe me that much, please?"

Sean didn't say anything. It didn't make sense. It wasn't possible. It was as if everything he was doing here was somehow flowing back to his house. There had to be some reasonable explanation.

"What was that about red dye?" asked Jimmy.

Jimmy! thought Sean. *What had he said earlier? The red dye would tell us something about the people who had built the pit?* And maybe it had.

He thought about all the spells he performed, over and over again. He always thought they hadn't worked, but what if in a way they had? What if they were building strength until they were strong enough to...?

Sean walked over to the pit and stared down at it. Like pieces of a puzzle, a picture began to form in his mind and he didn't like what he saw. No, he didn't like it at all. A cold breeze wafted through the trees, stirring the beads of sweat forming on his forehead.

First, the fires at the house, and then the journal page. Now the red dye was flowing back to Sean's house, the house where he had started performing dark magic. And how had he described his life? A nightmarish pit of despair? That's what he had always envisioned, how he had always thought of his life in that house. His mind went back to the moment he and the guys discovered the pit. They found it exactly when he was telling them about the Money Pit. It had been such a remarkable coincidence. But what if it wasn't a coincidence at all? What if they didn't find it? What if Sean accidentally created it? Is it possible that this pit was a physical manifestation of his darkest thoughts? A real pit of despair?

No, that's impossible! This is a real pit. It's not like I'm the only one that can see it. Jimmy, Tom, and Bear had spent weeks helping me excavate it. It's real, made of solid earth. This is all nonsense!

As if to answer to his thoughts, the water within the pit began to change. Once a placid pool of muddy water, before his eyes it rapidly turned into a thick blood-red liquid, churning and boiling angrily. The three boys automatically backed away from the edge of the pit as something moved below the surface of the water.

"Oh, man, look! Look!" yelled Bear, pointing into the pit.

Jimmy shrieked and pointed into the pit. "Oh my

God! Oh my God!"

There was something floating in the water. It was covered in the thick red liquid (*blood?*), and Sean didn't recognize what he was seeing at first. All he could tell for sure was that it looked pretty disgusting. Then it slowly dawned on him that what he was seeing was a human body. A headless human body!

No, I didn't do this! I couldn't have done this! Sean's mind screamed. His stomach churned violently, and he felt like all the air around him had been sucked away. Sean involuntarily gasped and choked.

"Tom! It's Tom!" yelled Jimmy.

"What? No way!" countered Bear.

"There! The jacket! That's the old army jacket he always wears! See the American flag on the shoulder? It's his 'Rocket's Red Glare' jacket!"

"Tom!" gasped Sean, now also recognizing the jacket. Jimmy was right. Tears began to stream down his face.

The argument!

And Sean knew. The pit had taken its first victim for him. Sean's spells had manifested into a monster, and every person who had ever wronged him would now feel the full wrath of all of his anger. He knew this now beyond any doubt.

I killed Tom! He was my friend and I killed him! I killed him! Sean barely noticed he was sobbing uncontrollably. *I have to stop this! But how? How?*

Jimmy and Bear were also crying. Sean looked at the grief etched into their faces and another sharp pain struck him in his gut.

What have I done? What have I done?

"What's going on over there?" shouted her sister through the phone.

Sean had forgotten about her.

"There's a scratching at the door," she said. "Is that you?"

Sean glanced at the wooden plaque on the ground.

The plaque with the three deep claw marks.

The Grishla! He realized. *If magic is real, then so is the Grishla!*

"Stephanie, no!" screamed Sean into the phone, turning to look at Tom's Rocket's Red Glare jacket, the only thing that he recognized of his friend—his friend who he had just killed. *You've killed your friend and now your magic is going after your family, Sean. You did this, you did this!* His mind accused. *You're killing everything in this world that you love.* "Stay away from the door! Stay away from the door!"

But all he heard at the other end of the line was an agonized wail.

Chapter Sixteen

Fumbling with his jacket pockets, Bear searched for his cell phone. He needed to pull himself together, call his father and get the police down here.

It's our fault, thought Bear. *We were a bunch of stupid kids digging a hole in the ground and we got our friend killed! We should have listened to Tom, damn it, why didn't we?*

Locating his phone, Bear punched in 911 and put the device to his ear. Nothing. Bear checked it was on and tried again. Still nothing. Then he saw he had no bars...but he'd never had trouble getting reception in the ravine before...

He looked to Sean who was somehow still talking to his sister. How was that possible? Sean had a direct line to his home in New York, yet he couldn't get through to the local police station?

There was an increase in bubbling, a gurgling in the water near Tom's body. Bear felt his muscles tense even though he wasn't sure why. A rush of unexplainable fear rose in his throat and threatened to choke off his breath.

"Hey, what is that?" asked Bear, nudging Jimmy.

Jimmy, he noted, had suddenly stopped crying. His face had turned into a distorted mask of shocked astonishment.

A reptilian head like an alligator's, yet different (*More like a Velociraptor on Jurassic Park,* thought

Bear) rose out of the red water. The head looked strange and mutated, bright red and appeared somehow melted. The eyes were white with no pupils, yet those eyes seemed fixed on Bear, and it let out an ungodly hiss.

Epilogue

Five Years Earlier – The Roanoke Colony Farm House
(Currently owned by Jimmy Cooper and occupied by his siblings and his Aunt Becky)

"They came a long way to die," said Vince, walking around the front of the truck, his suitcase in one hand and Kim's suitcase in the other.

"I doubt that's why they came up here," responded Kim, smiling at her little brother as he placed her bag at her feet.

Vince leaned against the side of the truck next to Kim and stared out across the field of tall golden grass that was bordered by maple trees with fiery orange and red leaves. Beyond the trees, the sunset was also ablaze with shocking pinks and deep burgundies. "So why did they come up here then? All the way up to freakin' Maine? The whole thing—this whole place—gives me the creeps."

Kim shrugged, "It *is* a mystery. But that's why we're here."

Vince yawned and stretched, his normally tidy, blonde pony-tail was set slightly askew, and escaping wisps of shimmering hair stuck out in every direction. Kim could tell the long drive had taken a toll on him, and she was glad they had reached their destination before dark. Absentmindedly, she ran her fingers through her own blonde hair, using her hand as a makeshift comb. The drive had been far too long for both of them.

"I hear they found baby Virginia the first day," he pointed out into the field at a dingy yellow tent that blended in with the golden grass. "Except, of course, she was a teenager when she died. Sad. I wonder if she knew that someday little grade-school children would be forced to memorize her name?"

Kim gave a short laugh. "You have such an interesting way of viewing things."

The two remained silent for a while, staring out at the scenery in front of them. There was something haunting about the small maple orchard. The grass and brittle leaves rustled as a breeze wafted through the landscape. To her left, Kim heard the musical notes of a wind chime, coming from the porch of the farmhouse. The day had been sunny, but the chill in the wind hinted at the coming snowstorm the radio weatherman had predicted earlier in the day.

So early in the season, Kim thought to herself. *Today is only Halloween! Or is it possible that this normal weather for Maine?*

As both remained silent and still, hypnotized by the New England landscape, the wind chime sounded again, and a disturbing thought entered Kim's mind.

Why can't I hear the birds? she wondered. *Or a*

dog or insects or something? It's so quiet...

"So what is all that stuff, wheat or something?" asked Vince, pointing to the field.

"Just ordinary grass," she responded with a laugh. "I think the guy just needs to mow..."

"Fire!" Vince suddenly yelled, pointing to the left. A plume of white could be seen coming from the field, partially blocked by the roof of the back porch.

Kim followed Vince as he broke into a run and bounded up the back porch steps. To her surprise, he abruptly came to a skidding stop, and Kim almost crashed into him.

"Here now, who are you two?" came the voice of an elderly man standing on the porch. "And what business do you have here on my property?"

The man was dressed in a pair of well-worn jeans and a faded blue shirt; his face was deeply lined and tanned from many years in the sun. He had a no-nonsense look about him, which suited Kim just fine. She could deal with his type.

"Actually, it isn't your property anymore," said Kim casually, sneaking a peak at the smoke, realizing it was now diminishing. "You're Nate Anderson, right? You sold the property to American Heritage Museum, our employer."

"Actually, young lady, I sold it to the owner of your museum, Richard King," he replied, a hint of anger in his voice. "Now there's an appropriate name if I ever heard one. The man thinks he is the King, eh?"

"Well...um..," stumbled Kim, but then stopped. She really couldn't say anything, Nate had a point. But bad-talking an employer as powerful and vindictive as Richard King was career- suicide, to say the least. The silence stretched on and the notes of a wind chime reached her ears. Kim could feel her face flush.

Nate smiled back at her, seeing he had made his point and continued, "In the old days, museums belonged to colleges or the National Trust. But not now...now they're owned by multi-billionaires." He then shook his head in apparent disgust. "Men with big money and little sense. I hear your boss owns businesses all over the world: Big oil, frackin', GMOs, chemicals—just about anything that makes money and destroys the planet. Am I right? Shame on both of you for working for that man."

"If you felt that way, sir, why did you sell him the land?" asked Kim, crossing her arms in a defiant gesture. "There are plenty of other museums out there."

"Well, now, that's my business, ain't it?" he snapped back.

"Sir...the fire..," continued Vince, pointing to the dissipating white smoke.

"Ay-yup," he said with a short nod. "Doused it with water. She's safe now. Besides, in another four hours or so she'll be covered with snow anyway."

Kim's eyes narrowed. Something about the whole situation seemed strange. "An odd time to burn leaves, isn't it?"

Nate sighed in exasperation. "Not leaves and nothin' to concern yourselves with. I was simply performing a Native American rite, transferring the property over to your boss." A little smile formed on his lips. "You make sure to tell your boss that, yah hear? The property is his now—*all* his, and everything that goes with it."

"I'm afraid we don't know him personally," said Kim, maintaining a sternness in her voice. There was something malicious about the old man. She didn't know what he was up to, but considering his animosity toward her employer, she'd be willing to bet it wasn't anything good.

The old man ignored her and walked to the edge of the porch, staring out across the field. Several long seconds passed before he spoke once more. "Bet'cha never thought you'd end up here. Who'd ever guess that the first British colony, the Roanoke Colony, would be discovered way up here in Maine? Bet'cha just about fell out of your chair when you heard, didn't yah?"

Vince laughed. "I'm not going to argue with that statement."

"And your family knew the whole time?" asked Kim. "Why didn't they tell anyone?"

He shrugged and walked back to them. "Why should we? History books don't need to know everything. The colonists hung up their boots here, and they deserve to rest in peace; 'nuff said."

On this reply, Kim wanted to scream. She spent years working at the Roanoke site, every day hoping to figure out what had happened to the lost colony. Yet Nate's family had been up here in Maine, sitting on the truth the whole time.

Why in the hell would someone do that? She wondered.

"So what changed your mind?" returned Vince, asking the most obvious question. "Why did your family decide to finally tell their story and sell the farm to a museum?"

"My wife and brother died, that's why." The old man pointed out across the field of grass at a tree, in the direction where he had been staring a moment earlier. "Right over there, under that tree. They found them there, torn apart by a cougar. Or so they said. About six months ago."

Kim gasped and pressed her hand to her mouth. The matter-of-fact manner in which he stated the gruesome tragedy left her ill-prepared for the shocking news.

"Dude...seriously?" asked Vince, his surfer accent from his youth accidentally slipping out.

"Ay-yup," Nate replied coldly.

Silence returned, and Kim looked back out at the tree. It had black, twisted bark with blood-red leaves. There were several raise lumps along the trunk, creating the illusion that it was diseased. She knew she had probably fallen under the spell of his disturbing story, but there was something very haunting and unsettling about that tree.

"My wife and I, we lived here quietly for many years. Then my brother showed up and got these ideas about digging up things." His face turned red with anger. "Greedy bastard. Got the two of them killed, he did."

Huh? Thought Kim, unable to follow his logic. *Did I miss something?*

"What does that have to do with a cougar attack?" asked Kim. "Would your wife have normally been inside of the house, is that what you mean?"

"And what did you mean by 'or so they said'?" asked Vince, with an uneasy look on his face. "Are you implying it wasn't a cougar attack?"

He's right, she thought. *That was an odd thing*

to say.

Nate crossed his arms and looked Kim and Vince up and down for a moment. "So what do the two of you do for your employer? You don't look like lawyers."

"No, sir, we work at the museum in North Carolina," answered Kim, ignoring the fact that he had changed the topic. The death of his wife and brother was no doubt a painful subject, and she saw no reason to continue discussing it. "We're anthropologists."

The smile on the man's face faded. "I was expecting a few suits to show up to take possession. I thought all of you 'ologist' people were done here until next summer."

"You mentioned some boxes in your basement last week," said Kim. "Said your family had records here, including some journals from family members about the find."

He nodded slowly. "Meant for the suits to come pick them up..."

"No suits today, sir," said Vince cheerfully, putting on a friendly smile. "Just us real people."

Kim knew Vince's words were meant to gain trust, but instead a grim expression hardened on the farmer's face.

"Anthropologists? Damn. I hadn't been expecting...you look like good kids, too," he muttered, looking very uncomfortable. His eyes in particular bothered Kim. Now that he knew who they were, he looked strangely uncertain. "Went through college and worked hard to get where you're at, didn't yah? Bet your parents are proud of you, right proud." Again he shook his head. "Nothin' for it. Can't undo what's been done.

No…can't undo it now…"

Once more, the old man looked out toward the tree, and his breathing grew rapid.

"Sir, I don't understand..," she began.

Nate turned back to them, making eye contact with both. His eyes were wide with what could only be described as urgency—and fear.

"I moved the boxes you're looking for up into the study on the second floor," he said quickly. "They're sitting next to the desk, and they're well marked. I placed my mother's journal on top of the desk. You'll be wanting to read that, an easier read than the original ones from the settlers."

"If you don't mind me asking sir," said Vince. "Why did you hold them back?"

True to form, Nate continued to ignore their questions, but this time he was nervously wringing his hands. Clearly, something had changed, and Kim was beginning to feel alarmed. "I left the electricity on so you could read the journals tonight. I also left you some firewood for the fireplace. There's an extra stack of firewood next to the house. But don't go after any more wood once night falls, yah hear? Dark is in about another half hour, so you better hurry up and get your things and what you'll need inside."

This guy is a nut case! She thought to herself. All she wanted now was for him to leave.

"Yes, yes, of course," she stammered, trying to think of a way to send him on his way. "You have a good evening. Best wishes…" she paused short, realizing that wishing him well on his new life that had been sparked by the death of his wife would be completely inappropriate. Instead she said, "And, sir, once again, my deepest

The Hunted Tribe: Rocket's Red Glare

condolences on the loss of your brother and wife."

Vince nodded. "Yeah...we had no idea," he added, his face turning slightly pink. "We apologize about intruding during this terrible time."

"I...I really had expected corporate types, lawyers and other similar vermin. Not a couple of kids. And a good pair you are, too. Polite. Listened to an old man's ramblings and even acknowledged his pain. Nope. Hadn't expected a couple of polite kids."

The man's face turned hard once more, and he took a step toward Kim and Vince.

"Stay in the house after dark!" Nate insisted. "As soon as it's light outside tomorrow, pack it up and hightail it out of here! There's nothing here beyond those three boxes, just take them and get yourselves home. I'd send you home now, but night time is too close, and I can't take you with me because you work for *him*, and I ain't taking that risk, no sir. I'm done with this. I've served my time!"

"Risk? What risk?" asked Kim.

Nate continued as though he hadn't heard her. "Make sure to lock up—all the locks, doors and windows!—and just hole up here for the night. And don't open the door for anyone, no matter who they say they are!"

Kim and Vince exchanged glances. Vince's expression of shock, no doubt mirrored her own.

"No matter who...you think we should be afraid of person?...I thought you said a cougar killed your brother and wife?" asked Vince.

The farmer huffed and then walked away from them. "There ain't no cougar around here," he called back. "There hasn't been any puma in these parts for a good ten years."

Nate stepped off the porch without looking back and disappeared around the house. A moment later they heard a car engine start and watched as a jeep drove away from the house.

Kim and Vance remained quiet, then turned their eyes back to the stand of maple trees.

"Like I said, this place gives me the creeps," grumbled Vince, shaking his head.

A movement near the trees suddenly caught Kim's attention, and she watched as an eerie ripple in the tall grass headed toward the house. Her muscles tightened, and she took a step back. *Is it an animal?* she wondered. *A cougar?* But then Kim noticed the haunting notes of the wind chime behind her die away and the grass stilled.

Only the wind. She breathed a sigh of relief. *You're an idiot, Kim. He was just trying to give you a good scare!*

"Let's try not to get ourselves spooked here," she answered finally, mentally chastising herself for letting the old man play her. "We've got a long night ahead of us."

"Yeah," laughed Vince, shaking his head. "In a freaky old house, during a huge snowstorm, a few yards from where two people were torn apart by some wild animal. Oh, yes, and let's not forget that an entire colony perished here, for some unknown reason, centuries back."

Kim gave a slight laugh. "The perfect Halloween night, don't you think?"

Vince's eyes grew wide. "Do you think that's all it was, that stuff about his wife and brother? A Halloween prank?"

"Seems pretty likely, don't you think?" she said with a reassuring grin, almost more for herself than for Vince. The last thing she wanted to do was to let her little brother see her rattled. Kim knew she had to pull it together. "Besides, we're both pretty tough. We're from the bad part of Miami, remember? Carjackings and drive-by shootings were an everyday occurrence where we used to live. This is the country. I'm sure we're safer here than where we grew up."

Vince let out an unexpected laugh and pointed to the house. "You sure about that?"

Kim turned around to see where he was pointing, and her jaw dropped open.

All the windows and doors were covered with the thickest security bars she had ever seen.

"Trick or Treat," muttered Vince quietly.

***

Kim placed two grocery bags on the dining-room table just as Vince trotted down the stairs.

"I put your suitcase in the pink room as you requested," said Vince, as he entered the kitchen. "Is that the last of it?"

Kim nodded, a look of concern on her face. "I turned on the radio in the car when I was looking to make sure we hadn't forgot anything. They're predicting a pretty big storm. They said to have supplies for several days…"

"Oh," uttered Vince weakly.

"Yeah, 'oh'," she returned, hoping he grasped the gravity of the situation.

Vince began to rummage through the two grocery bags. "Let's see…two sandwiches, two tiny bags of potato chips and a box of granola bars...I don't think that qualifies as 'supplies for several days'." He then chuckled, reached into the second bag and pulled out her coffeemaker. "But hey...thank heaven, you remembered to bring this from home and a bag of your freshly-ground espresso. With enough of a caffeine buzz, we'll forget all about those hunger pangs, right?"

"Ha-ha," she groaned, taking the coffeemaker from him and placing it down on the table. "And it's the holiday blend today, by the way; no espresso."

Vince sighed, yawned then stretched. "Well, as much as I hate to get back in the pickup, it looks like I need to make another trip to that local store we spotted a few miles back."

Inside, Kim felt herself cringe as the words of the old man echoed in her skull.

Vince gave her a sideways glance, catching her change in mood. "Oh, don't worry, Mother Hen. It's not that far. Besides, my truck is a little big for that cougar to attack."

Kim was vigorously shaking her head now, an unreasonable fear rising into her throat. "A storm is coming and night is about to fall, and you want to jump back in the truck and drive around on a dark, winding country road?" she argued. "What if you get lost? What if you miss a turn? You'd be out there in a blizzard waiting for a tow truck! It's too dangerous."

"Dangerous and futile," came a voice from behind them.

Kim and Vince both whirled around. While bringing in the two grocery bags, Kim had left open the front door. Now a tall man stood in the doorway, wearing a black leather jacket and a wide-rim hat. It took Kim a few heartbeats to realize the man was wearing a sheriff's uniform under his jacket. In relief, she let out a pent up breath of air.

"Sorry to startle you, folks. Sheriff James McKinney," he said as he touched the brim of his hat in an informal nod of hello. "Heard you folks were coming up here from the museum to check up on the Roanoke site. I was worried you might not be prepared for the coming snowstorm."

"You guessed right," remarked Vince, walking toward the sheriff, hand extended. "My name is Vince Molina, and this is my sister, Kim."

Kim offered her hand and added, "Dr. Kim Molina. And very soon my brother will also be able to use that title. He just finished his doctorate."

Vince blushed and looked down. It embarrassed him when she did this, but she didn't care. When he hit 21, the whole family thought he would end up a permanent beach-bum. They were all so proud of how he'd turned his life around and was now following in his big sister's footprints.

The sheriff shook their hands and seemed to suppress a laugh at the family drama. Kim noted his rusty-brown skin, high cheekbones and dark, penetrating eyes. *Native American?* she wondered.

"You two are a little out of your element up here," the sheriff said. "I'm assuming you two live near Roanoke Island way down south and were working that site before this?"

They nodded.

"Yep, don't quite get the snowstorms down

there that they get up here in Maine," he said with a laugh.

"Is it true about the storm?" asked Kim nervously, trying hard to resist the urge to chew on her nails, a childhood habit that she found very difficult to break. "Do you think we'll be snowed in for a few days?"

"I'm afraid those are the facts, ma'am. And from the sound of it, it's going to be a real apple-shaker. But going to the store isn't the best idea. Earl closed up the store about a half-hour ago, to get ready for the storm."

"Ah, hell..," grumbled Vince, rubbing his temples.

A broad smile stretched across the sheriff's face. "Have no fear, I picked up a few bags of basic groceries for you. Kind of had a feelin' you wouldn't be prepared."

Kim instantly wanted to hug the man. "Thank you so much!"

"No need to thank me, I just hate getting emergency calls during blizzards," He then turned to Vince and pointed his finger at him as though his hand were a derringer. "I especially don't like to work search and rescue in a white-out. You stay inside, yah here?"

Vince nodded, smiling broadly. "You'll get no argument from me, sir."

There was a slight pause, and the sheriff's face grew concerned.

"If you don't mind me asking, I overheard the two of you talking about that cougar attack earlier. I take it old Nate brought it up, did he?"

Kim and Vince nodded, and the officer groaned.

"He hasn't been quite the same since his wife and brother died. He took it pretty hard, I'm afraid. I thought he was on the path to recovery, selling the place and leaving to make a new life for himself. I had hoped this meant he was getting his feet on the ground again, but clearly from his conversation with you two he's back in la-la land again."

"He implied it wasn't a cougar," said Vince, with a nervous laugh.

The officer nodded. "Of course it was a cougar. Unfortunately, he attributed it to the local legend of..," he paused, clearly trying to decide if he should tell them. Finally, with a sigh, he continued. "...the legend of the Lizard Man."

Kim choked. "Excuse me?"

The officer smiled, but his expression remained serious. "Afraid so. One of the more colorful stories around here, kind of our version of bigfoot. Sadly, many people believe in it. Nate claimed the creature killed his brother and wife for digging up the Roanoke secret. Apparently, they wanted the family secret to come out, wanted to tell the world about the Roanoke colony."

"And the Lizard Man wouldn't like that?" asked Vince, grinning.

"Ay-yup. The Lizard Man was, according to Nate, the one that killed the colonists way back when. Followed them all the way up from Roanoke Island."

Now Kim laughed. She'd studied ancient religions, but a Lizard Man was a new one for her. She then felt her face flush as the officer stared at her with a stony face. Finally, he gave her a dismissive wave.

"It's ok, I don't expect you to believe it; can't say I do either. But I can tell you Nate believed it and so did all of his kin. So much so they kept a lid on the Roanoke colony. They could have made a fortune selling the story and artifacts, but they didn't. They feared the Lizard Man too much. Mind you, none of us knew about the colonists, and I have no idea why the Lizard Man would target these poor people. But that's the legend."

"Holy freakin' Iguana," laughed Vince once more, shaking his head.

The officer's eyes darkened, and Kim felt a shiver.

"What?" Vince asked. "There's something you're not telling us."

Officer McKinney nodded. "Nate believed in the curse; I mean truly, in his heart, down to the pit of his soul, believed it. When his wife and brother supposedly activated the curse he had bars installed on all the windows and doors. Told me he knew he were a dead man if he didn't get out from under the curse. Said the only way he could do that was to transfer the curse to someone else. Apparently, his family had been sitting on a Native American ceremony that would perform the transfer, but didn't use it. They didn't want to bring harm to someone else. Nate, however, had developed a different view. He said he chose your boss because he's an evil man. Said 'let monsters beget monsters.' And coming up your steps, I noticed a ceremonial circle burned into the back lawn. Looks fairly fresh."

"So you're here to warn us that the Lizard Man's out to get us, is that it?" remarked Vince, a lilt of humor in his voice.

Kim, however, felt a little queasy as she picked up on the officer's true message. "It's Nate you're worried about, isn't it? Do you think he'll come back and mess with us?"

Vince dropped his smile. Clearly, this thought had not occurred to him.

"I sure hope not, Ma'am, but he's not exactly thinking clearly right now. I'd keep your doors locked. Don't open it up no matter who you hear out there." He pulled out his card and gave it to them. "Call me if he shows up. I mean it."

Kim eagerly took his card.

"You know, it's funny, but what you said just now is almost word for word what Nate told us," said Vince. "I wondered about that at the time. Cougars don't typically knock on people's front doors and pretend to be your long lost cousin."

"Legend has it the Lizard Man can imitate people for short periods of time."

Vince gasped and in a mock voice said, "And how do we know you're not the Lizard Man? How do we know you're not going to drag us outside and eat us?"

The officer seemed caught off guard by this absurd accusation and let out an abrupt chuckle. Quickly, though, he regained his composure, then focused a pair of intense brown eyes back on Vince. "Son, I'm the sheriff in these parts. Do you know what that means?"

A thoughtful expression crossed Vince's features for a moment. "Your duty is to protect and serve?"

"Nope, it means I have a gun," he said, pointing to his revolver that was tucked away in the gun holster around his waist. "Which means if I wanted someone dead I'd just shoot them and bury them in the woods." As though wanting to see if his words had achieved the desired impact, he waited a brief moment, then added, "Besides, my wife has me on a plant-based diet right now. No eating the tourists."

Kim and Vince both broke out laughing, and the officer joined in.

"Come on. Let's get those groceries out of my car. I need to get going. I have a homemade mushroom pot pie waiting for me."

***

Within an hour, the two siblings had set up operations upstairs in the study. A warm fire crackled in an enormous stone fireplace behind an antique fire-screen; the radio, sitting next to the open journals on a huge, ornately carved mahogany desk, played an endless loop of Halloween music, briefly punctuated by ghost stories; Kim's electric coffee-pot percolated on a small end-table, the warm, inviting scent of spiced coffee filling the room.

Kim and Vince sat in a pair of matching leather wingback chairs, enjoying their sandwiches and chips. Scanning the room, she was stunned at their surroundings. She had expected the study to match the rest of the house, decorated in cheerful yellows and faded French-blue toile patterns. Instead, this room looked like something from an old murder mystery. Antiques, dark wood, dusty books, and red walls surrounded them. Everything was so very British, so very grave and dower, that she half expected to hear the hounds outside,

The Hunted Tribe: Rocket's Red Glare

baying on the moors. In the meantime, Vince, always oblivious to everything except satisfying his needs, rummaged around for an object on the coffee-table. Without asking, Kim knew beyond a shadow of a doubt what he was looking for.

"Ah-ha!" he declared, holding up a black, rectangular object in his hands. "I found the TV remote!"

"I'm so thrilled for the both of you," snickered Kim. "I'm sure the two of you will be very happy together."

"I'm sure we will, too," he said, giving the remote a big kiss.

Vince clicked the remote and the large flat screen on the wall lit up to a shriek of velociraptors.

"Wonderful," groaned Kim. "Just what we need right now. *Jurassic Park*. I'm sure the Lizard Man is pleased."

Vince laughed and turned the channel. Next came up a *Godzilla* movie, then another click and some unknown black and white movie with dinosaurs and cowboys appeared, another click and the second *Jurassic Park* movie showed up on the screen.

"Wow," muttered Vince, clicking the remote again, and the first *Jurassic Park* movie once again appeared on the screen. "People in Maine sure like their dinosaurs. I wish this set got cable. Only four damn channels..."

"Forget that," she said, crumpling up her sandwich wrapper and tossing it into the trash. "I'm more interested in the journal. Ancient mysteries tonight, ancient movies another day."

He shrugged and turned off the TV. "Sounds

like a plan."

The two wandered back to the large desk where the journal written by Nate's mom had been laid out for them, already opened up to an entry. Kim turned off the radio and sat down in the leather chair behind the desk. Vince pulled up another chair next to her and also settled in.

"Check it out," she said, pointing to colorful sticky notes poking out of the pages. "He didn't want us to just read her journal, he wanted us to read specific sections."

"He's definitely trying to send us a message," groaned Vince. "I don't know how helpful this is going to be."

"I doubt it will be helpful at all," said Kim. "However, it's Halloween night, and we might as well enjoy Nate's ghost story."

"Ah, yes, a ghost story from the mind of a madman," laughed Vince. "I guess that is a good one for Halloween, isn't it?"

Kim picked up the book and began to read, starting on the first page that was marked with a neon-pink sticky note:

"Sept. 6, 1950 - Amelia Anderson.'

"I am beginning this journal for my newborn child, Nate, to help him understand the curse that he has inherited upon his birth. My dear Nate, I wish I could spare you from this. But it is part of our family, and you will now be handed the curse as I have. It will be your duty to educate your children, as it is my duty to educate you now."

"Nice," said Vince, shaking his head. "Welcome to the world—FYI, you're going to live your whole life under a curse."

As usual, Kim ignored his sarcastic

commentary. "My dearest boy, it is imperative that you take the curse seriously. For if anyone breaks the rules, the curse shall be triggered, and you will not escape with your life."

"So like the Sheriff said, he has a curse, but it hasn't been activated yet," asked Vince, sitting back in his chair, arms crossed.

"Well, not when she wrote this," said Kim, turning the pages. "Sounds like he believes it has been now, though."

Vince turned to her with his eyebrows scrunched together in his trademark annoyed expression. "What are you doing? She just started..."

Momentarily pausing her page-turning to flick a sticky-note with her index finger, she replied, "There's a note saying to go to the next marked page," she continued turning pages until she reached the next sticky note, marked "No. 2."

Once more, Kim began to read: "My family kept the journals of the Roanoke colony so the family would never forget the details of the curse. While other families listened to the radio at night, my father read from the colonists' journals to the entire family every night. I envied the other families, but knew our survival depended upon this information."

"They believed in it that much?" asked Vince, stunned. "Religious families don't read from their bible as often as that. Every night?"

"What would that do to the children, listening to horror stories of a curse every night?" muttered Kim. "This is almost child abuse!"

"You know, we're not just reading about a family curse here," said Vince. His eyes held a glint of alarm. "We're reading about Nate's descent into madness. He never really stood a chance. I'm glad he found a way to escape the family curse, even if he was just fooling himself. I just hope he isn't so far gone that he comes back here to reenact the curse on us!"

Kim nodded and continued to read: "The language in the journals is very old and difficult. As a child, I listened to these stories so often I began to take on their way of speaking. To spare you the ridicule that I endured, Nate, I will translate the legends into a more modern tongue."

Kim turned the pages to Note 3. "Finally," she said, pulling the note free and showing it to Vince. The note said clearly: 'Roanoke Colony: The Beginning of the Curse.'

Vince sat up straight in his chair and placed his hand on Kim's wrist. "After all these years—we'll finally know…"

Kim shook her head. "The Lizard Man, remember? That's what Nate thinks it is, remember?"

Vince sighed and fell back against his chair-back in disgust. "Oh, yeah. Damn. Ok, on with the fairy tale."

Kim began to read: "It was on the very day that the leader of the colony left for more supplies that our hunting party brought back a wounded man. One of the native people from a distant tribe, far up north called the Dwanake."

"The Dwanake?" said Vince. "Who the hell were they?"

Kim looked back at him startled. "But Native American heritage is your main focus. You've never heard of them?"

Vince shrugged his shoulders. "Probably a small tribe that died out from smallpox or something. It happened a lot back then."

Kim sighed sadly and then continued reading. "The man had been attacked by a creature. He had three terrible claw marks across his body, the spread indicating that it was a single paw or talon, stretched 12 inches across. The man, however, refused to say what attacked him. It was only later that men from the Croatoan tribe, a priest and a conjuror (a man who spoke to animal spirits) came to warn us that the man lived under a curse for wronging one of the animal spirits known as the Grishla."

Kim glanced at Vince, who returned a puzzled expression. He then reached over and took the journal from Kim, skimming the pages with his index finger.

"What?" she asked.

After a moment, Vince returned the book to her, leaned back in his chair and crossed his arms. "Well...they're not wrong about the Croatoan religion. They had a priest and a conjuror, and it was the job of the conjuror to speak to animal spirits. So far, they have their facts straight. Never heard of a Grishla, though. This sounds promising. Keep reading."

Kim continued. "The Grishla was a very reclusive and powerful animal spirit. Few knew of its existence, and those who did, knew not to speak its name. For to speak its name was the same as calling it out, and the Grishla does not like to be disturbed."

"Grumpy little cuss," muttered Vince, tossing one of the crumbled notes in the air like a ball, catching it and re-catching it as he listened.

"It was an ancient lizard that once ruled the world, long before man existed. As I heard stories about dinosaurs, I wondered if this creature was the same. Of course, this was not possible because it was described as having feathers, and in fact, used its feathered tail to hypnotize its victims. As we all know, dinosaurs do not have feathers."

Vince let out a choked laugh and dropped his makeshift paper ball to the floor. "Holy Jurassic Attacks!"

Kim also laughed in disbelief. "That's amazing! How could the Native Americans of that time know that the dinosaurs had feathers?" asked Kim, startled.

"The same way we do," answered Vince. "Archaeopteryx. The feathers were embedded in the surrounding mud when the creature died and impressions were fossilized into the stone. It's not out of the realm of possibilities that they found a similar specimen. Keep reading...I'm just getting into this."

"Oh, ok," grumbled Kim, picking up the book again. Her brother was taking some of the fun out of their spooky legend with his cold, hard facts. "The Dwanake angered the creature when their conjurors tried to enslave the Grishla so they could use it to wage war on their neighbors. Ever since that day, the Dwanake have been known as 'The Hunted Tribe,' as that is what they became. Always on the run, always hiding from the creature who swore to kill every member and descendant of the tribe."

"Yep, grumpy lizard indeed," laughed Vince.

"The members of the tribe scattered across the

land. Many attempted to hide in other tribes, claiming to belong to a different people than their own and marrying into the host tribe. But all who knowingly help the Dwanake escape their fate, will also be subjected to a different curse. They must hand over the accursed party to the Grishla and hide all evidence of the existence of the Grishla, the Dwanake tribe, and the victims. If the cursed parties die, the land where they die becomes cursed, and the new landowner will be subjected to the same curse, forced to hide all evidence of those who died. If the land is sold, the curse will be transferred to the new owner, but only if the original owner performs the proper ceremonies.'

"The Roanoke Colony, regretfully, tried to hide the man rather than hand him over to the creature. A woman who possessed knowledge of witchcraft used her skills to battle the creature, but lost. Many died. The Roanoke Colony refused to hand over the Dwanake tribesman, which enraged the creature, and a curse was placed on all members of the colony. The Roanoke Colony traveled north to try to find the original homelands of the Dwanake tribe, to free themselves of the curse. However, the Grishla caught up with them, and they were killed in a terrible slaughter on our farmland.'

"Our ancestors learned of the curse only after purchasing the land and discovering the journals. After many deaths and terrible encounters with the Grishla, they gave in to the conditions of the curse and hid all evidence of the colonists.'

"From the journals, we learned of the ceremony to transfer the curse to another; however, what good Christian would force this fate upon another?"

"Your dear boy Nate, that's who," laughed Vince. "His mother is probably spinning in her grave as we speak."

Kim nodded. "There's more, of course. I actually left out a few references to other areas in the journal with more detailed information, but it's all a silly fairy tale."

"Maybe or maybe not," said Vince. "They got the Croatoan religion right. And I've met some very solid, salt-of-the-earth tribesmen who swear that animal spirits are real."

Kim laughed but then saw Vince wasn't. "Are you kidding me? *You* believe in the Lizard Man now?"

Vince shrugged. "I'm just saying I'm not 100% convinced animal spirits aren't real."

Kim stood up and stretched. "Yeah, but when was the last time you heard of an animal spirit attacking someone? And a dinosaur animal spirit at that? Seriously?"

"Reclusive, she said," he remarked. "Maybe the other tribes didn't know about..."

Vince's words abruptly stopped as a bright light flashed through the window.

"What in the world?" asked Kim, turning toward the light.

Vince leapt to his feet and ran to the window. "Motion detector. Something's outside."

Following her brother, she tried to peek out the window, but was only met with the reflection of her own frightened face. Vince reached over and flipped off the wall switch, casting the room into darkness. Kim's reflection vanished, and the world outside emerged.

The motion-detector lights illuminated the field of grass and maple trees in an eerie blue light, changing the world outside into an alien landscape. Further obscuring their view, a scattering of snowflakes began to fall, announcing the arrival of the predicted storm. Eventually, Kim's eyes adjusted, and she could see something moving through the tall grass.

"It's just the wind," said Kim, remembering earlier in the day when she saw something similar.

Vince shook his head. "Wind doesn't trigger motion detectors."

"Oh...A coyote then?" she asked. *Not a cougar,* she thought to herself. *Please don't say a cougar...*

Vince's mouth pressed into a thin line. "Hard to tell. That grass is as tall as me, maybe taller. It could even be a man down there.

Kim's breath caught in her throat at these words. Leaning closer to the glass, she watched the steady motion of the object, moving around the yellow tent covering the dig site. The object then stopped and abruptly turned left, deliberately making its way toward the house. For a moment, Kim felt a wave of panic pass through her.

Whatever or whoever it is, it's coming here!

Kim's terrified face suddenly reappeared in the window as bright light and sound unexpectedly erupted in the room behind them, and both Vince and Kim yelped and whirled around. It was the television set. The device had turned on, showing a scene from one of the dinosaur movies. Coincidentally, the scene was of men walking through tall grass and creatures sneaking up behind them, leaving deep furrows in the grass—very similar to the scene in the backyard below.

"Would you turn that stupid thing off?" hissed Kim to Vince.

Vince's eyes were wide with surprise as he shook his head. "What are you talking about? I didn't turn it on to begin with. The remote is on the coffee-table where I left it. Besides, that's not even the channel I left it on!"

Kim glanced toward the table, but in the faint light of the television set she could only make out an outline around the table's perimeter. Anything sitting on top of it was still hidden in darkness. "You must be wrong, it's in your pocket or some..."

One of the dinosaurs on the TV set let out a high pitched shriek and leapt onto a screaming man. Kim cringed; she hated these kind of movies. Then, just as abruptly as it started, the TV screen went black.

To her right, Kim heard movement, and she involuntarily jumped. Another bright flash blinded her as Vince flipped on the lights. He ran back to the coffee-table and lifted up the remote.

"You see? I didn't have it. It was way over here!"

Kim felt a tremor in her hands as her nerves began to jitter. "No...that's not possible! And what of it anyway? Are you trying to tell me that a dinosaur animal spirit—what did they call it, 'the Grishla'—did this?"

"Actually, I have a worse idea than that," he said, looking a little pale.

"W...worse?" she stumbled over the word.

"What could be worse?"

"Well, for starters, what if old Nate is crazier than even the sheriff knew? What if the entire house is rigged?" asked Vince. "There are bars on the windows downstairs. The question is: Did he put the bars on the windows to keep something out or are the bars there to keep something in—namely us! Is it possible that he rigged this entire house to be our own personal Halloween fright house?"

Just then they heard the sound of footfalls as someone—or something—walked across the back porch.

***

The two siblings stood in the living-room, staring at the back door. They could hear something on the other side of the door, snuffling at the bottom like a dog. Occasionally, they'd hear an exploratory scratching. Other than this, they heard no other noise except the wind and snow buffeting the house.

Between the living room and the entryway, Kim had closed and locked another set of security bars, yet somehow, she still didn't feel safe.

"If it was Nate, why would he have the second gate?" asked Kim. "Even if something busts down the door, this gate will keep us safe."

Vince sighed as he made his way to a side window. Remaining low, he tried to peak through the lower corner. "Wouldn't mean much if he has his own set of keys, now would it? It could be just a trick to make us think we're safe. And FYI, I still can't make out whatever it is from the windows. All I can see is a moving shadow."

"Get away from the window, if he has a shotgun or something he could blow out the glass," said Kim while fishing through her pockets. She felt the small rectangle of thick stock paper. She latched onto it and pulled it out, then waved the card at Vince. "Here. Let's call the sheriff. I've still got his card."

She picked up the receiver to the house phone and placed it to her ear, then growled in exasperation.

"Let me guess, no dial tone," asked Vince, still peering out the window, ignoring her warnings. "He wouldn't be much of a psycho if it worked, now would he?"

"My cell is in the study. Be right back," answered Kim, then turned and ran up the stairs.

Within moments, she reached the top landing and made her way down the long hallway and into the study. She picked up her cell phone from the antique desk and quickly dialed the sheriff's number.

"Jim speaking," came the husky voice that she remembered from earlier.

"Good evening Sheriff McKinney, this is Kim Molina from the Roanoke dig site."

"Uh-oh," responded the man, concern in his voice. "Trouble already?"

"Umm...I'm not sure," Kim felt embarrassed now. No one had knocked at the door or turned the knob. So what would she say? The animal spirit of a dinosaur was scratching to get in? But she had to do something. Strange or not, they had some kind of situation on their hands. Screwing up her courage, she swallowed hard and pushed forward. "There's some kind of animal outside snuffling at the back door. We can't tell what it is..."

"Oh heck!" exclaimed the Sheriff. "Nate had a dog, Blue. Shoot, did he leave him behind? Oh, man, and that storm out there is fierce!"

Kim felt herself snap back to reality. *A dog? She recalled the snuffling at the door and it all fell into place. Of course, it was just a dog!*

"Look, Kim, I don't know how you feel about animals, but Blue is a good dog if there ever was one. Do you think you could let him in for the night? You can even put him in the basement if you want. He's an older fellow, and I know he just won't make it out there tonight."

Relieved, Kim let out a laugh and walked out of the study into the hall to tell Vince. "Of course! Of course! I can't tell you how much better I feel. I can't believe I actually thought it was the animal spirit of a stupid dinosaur..."

"Stupid?!" suddenly squawked the voice on the phone.

She stopped dead in her tracks, her mind confused. She had expected a startled reaction over the word 'dinosaur' or 'animal spirit' but not on the word 'stupid'. *Maybe I misunderstood what he said?* She wondered.

Suddenly, she heard the house phone ringing downstairs.

Is the house phone working again? she asked herself. *How odd...*

"Stupid? Stupid?" continued the sheriff on her cell phone, interrupting her train of thought. "You listen to me, lady. Maybe I was born just a 'stupid' animal, but that was a long time ago. I've had sixty-five million years to evolve, and I'm far smarter than any of you balding apes, that's for sure. And believe me when I say, it's been a long time since I needed to use my tail feathers to hypnotize my victims!"

For a moment, she shook her head. *What did he say? Is this a joke?* And then a choking fear rose into her throat. The sheriff had no way of knowing about the Grishla hypnotizing its victims with its tail feathers. She only knew about it because she read it in the journal a few minutes ago. He'd only know about it if...

"Nate!" she yelled into the phone, making sure her voice sounded angry, not afraid. There was no way in hell she was going to give him that satisfaction. "Who do you think..."

"Do you want to know what else is really stupid?" continued the voice. "Two college grads who don't bother to check their cell phones. Because if you had, you might have noticed you haven't had any cell reception since you arrived!"

Abruptly, the phone went dead.

Kim pulled the phone away from her ear and looked down at it.

No bars, none at all.

Her mind raced, trying to understand what had just happened. She made the call, so how could it have been Nate? And how does someone disable the reception to another person's cell phone?

"Hey, Sis!" called Vince from downstairs, followed by what sounded like the jingling of the security door. "That was the sheriff on the landline. Guess the phone is working again. He called to check in on us and told me that the animal at the door is probably just Nate's old dog, Blue, and

I should let him in."

Kim gasped.

"Vince, NO!!!" she yelled, running down the hallway.

Before she could reach the top stair landing she heard the door open, quickly followed by a pained cry and the ferocious shrieks of some terrible beast. Kim charged down the stairs in a blind panic. *This is impossible!* her mind screamed. *This can't be happening!* Her heart pounded in her chest as she made it to the bottom landing and ran into the living room.

Once there, she skidded to a stop.

The back door lay wide open, a relentless wind blowing in heavy amounts of snow and the security door between her and the back door was closed. At first she thought Vince had gone outside, but then saw him lying on the floor in the entry way, partially concealed behind the security door and the snow that was already beginning to pile up on the floor. His head lay against the security door, and as she grew closer, she could see a puddle of blood seeping under the door.

"Vince?" she said in a near whisper as she approached him.

"Stay back," he groaned in a raspy voice. "It's still here."

Kim looked around the entry room bewildered. He was alone, she would swear to it. But then she noticed movement. Around her brother was a floating cloud of red mist, glowing and throbbing. Something about the way it moved seemed menacing and intelligent.

The mist began to change. First the color turned darker, and then it grew denser. A form began to take shape. She couldn't believe what she was seeing. A dinosaur—a velociraptor!—stood over her brother. The creature rose slowly and looked at her with glowing red eyes. It was remarkable, beyond anything she could have ever imagined. It looked more like a parrot than a dinosaur with its blue skin and bright aquamarine and yellow feathers.

Something inside of her changed: Fear—terrible, and uncontrollable terror—rose inside of her. Every instinct she possessed screamed at her to run and hide.

Except she couldn't. *Vince! I'm not leaving my brother!*

Visions of their life together flashed in her mind. Their childhood romping on the beach and dark, stormy nights playing board games; Kim helping Vince with his studies to get ahead at school and her joy when he decided to take up anthropology; the two of them working side by side, planning out their careers together and securing their positions at the museum.

The dinosaur moved again, and Kim's attention snapped back to the present. With a bird-like jerk, the thing titled its head down and gazed sideways at Vince's prone body.

"No, please..," she whimpered.

With lightning speed, the dinosaur's head shot down, and the creature sunk its teeth into Vince's head. Vince screamed and his arms flailed, but with a sudden jerk to the right and the sound of breaking bones, his cry cut short and his arms dropped to the wood floor with a thud. The dinosaur released its hold and Vince's head dropped sideways, dangling at an impossible

The Hunted Tribe: Rocket's Red Glare

angle, as though his head and neck were now only attached by skin and muscle.

The creature abruptly vanished. Kim couldn't move, she couldn't think, none of it felt real. *Is this a dream?* She wondered. *It has to be! I fell asleep in the study, and I only have to wake up to make it all end. That has to be it!*

And then it was back. The Grishla reappeared at the doorway, reached down, latched onto Vince's right leg and rapidly pulled her brother's limp, broken body out the back door. Her brother's lifeless eyes stared at her as he disappeared into the darkness.

Vince was gone.

Kim watched silently as the snow continued to blow in the front door, turning into a red slush as it mixed with the blood. All of those years, all of those long hours working to discover what had happened to the colonists. It had been their dream. Vince and Kim had obsessed on it for years. Now, in this old house in Maine, the two of them discovered the truth together.

The price: her brother's life.

Kim dropped to her knees and began to sob.

***

Sitting quietly in one of the wingback chairs in the study and bundled up in a quilt, Kim's eyes were fixed on the television screen while she chewed on her nails and wiped away the tears rolling down her cheeks. On entering the study, she had pushed a heavy bookcase onto the floor in front of the door. It would take some work to move it in the morning, but right now, all she cared about was surviving the night.

She stared at the screen, watching a cheerful old musical and was grateful the television stations were no longer playing the dinosaur movies. Kim didn't want to think about the past few hours. All she wanted to do was stare at the television set and pretend that she was home—and that her brother was still alive.

As the Technicolor pictures flashed across the screen, however, her mind began to drift. Within a few seconds, in spite of her best efforts, she found herself mentally going over the events from earlier in the evening. The scientist in her quickly took over, and Kim began to compare what happened to Vince to what she had read in the journals. It seemed impossible, but she saw it all with her own two eyes: The Roanoke legend was real—the Grishla existed.

She pulled the quilt tightly around herself as an involuntary shudder passed through her body. *What's keeping the creature out of the house?* she wondered. *A cloud of mist can't be held back by bars. It doesn't make any sense! Nate was the one who had put the bars on the windows to keep the creature out, but maybe he didn't know it could turn into a cloud of mist? It was certainly possible.*

Kim pulled the quilt up to her chin, wanting to hide under it.

She wondered for a moment if the sheriff they met in person earlier in the day was the Grishla. *Didn't the sheriff say that according to the legend it could temporarily take human form? Was that the creature's way of mocking them by telling them this?* After a moment's consideration, she dismissed this possibility. He brought them groceries. How many dinosaur animal spirits have bank accounts and go grocery shopping?

Surprising herself with the absurd mental image, she gave a short, hysterical laugh and then immediately broke down into a choked sob. Kim gulped in a few gasps of air and forced back the tears. She needed to think clearly, she needed to keep her head and think this through.

"So why did it want Vince to open the door?" she muttered to herself, as she watched a woman in a beautiful red dress dancing with a man in a tuxedo. The scene was so serene and beautiful that Kim couldn't pull her eyes away. The movie was helping her calm her jangled nerves, and she was grateful for that small mercy. "It can't be the bars...they couldn't possibly keep the creature out. Is it some Native American spell?" A few more seconds played out as the couple continued to spin around the dance floor. It was really such a lovely picture. "Or is the answer simpler than that? Does the creature like to play with its prey, like a cat plays with a mouse? Is it possible that it could always get in the house any time it wanted? Even now?

These words should have sent her into a panic, yet the sharp sting of terror did not come. Kim leaned back in her chair and sighed as the romantic couple finally kissed and the words 'The End' flashed over them. She felt an odd peace spread over her.

"All that stupid stuff it said on the phone, too," muttered Kim, mindlessly watching the credits scroll by, wondering why even the credits brought her some odd type of comfort. "What kind of dinosaur uses a cell phone anyway?" She paused, remembering what it had said. "It is an evolved dinosaur, that's what it said, right? And what was that last thing it said?"

The screen was black now, but Kim noted she felt the same feelings of warmth and comfort filling her heart. *Where are the commercials? Or the next movie...or something?*

"It said, 'It's been years since I had to hypnotize my prey with my tail feathers'. So, what does an evolved, modern-day dinosaur spirit hypnotize its prey with these days, I wonder?"

She sighed, waiting for another show to start. Like most of the TV generation, Kim was mindlessly staring at the screen. *Hypnotized...*

Kim cried out and turned toward the door, except her view was blocked by a reptilian head. The creature was standing next to her—right next to her!—its glowing red eye glaring down at her in a predatory fashion. Its lips pulled back as it growled, exposing sharp, vicious teeth.

***

CBN (World News)
November 2nd - Las Vegas, Nevada

On the night of November 1st, Richard King, CEO of King Enterprise, and his six-member board of directors were mauled to death by an unidentified animal in his penthouse suite during a late-night board meeting. No one knows how a wild animal entered or left the penthouse or why Mr. King called the late night board meeting.

In a seemingly unrelated incident, on the previous night an employee of Mr. King's American Heritage Museum was also mauled by an animal at a remote farmhouse in Maine and another employee at the same site has gone missing. Authorities are investigating.

To be continued in

Hunted Tribe 3: Weapons of War

Thanks again to all of my readers and hope you enjoyed this book. Please visit my website http://trickortreatthrillers.com/ for more updates on my future books.

About the Author

Roma Gray is a huge fan of Halloween and has been writing horror, sci-fi, thrillers, and mysteries since she was eight years old. When she was thirteen she wrote her first novel. She currently livesin Oregon, in a haunted house with a ghost cat by the name of Koko, and four "living" friends, Nicky (orange tom cat), Roanoke (black cat), Cricket (Chihuahua), and Buttercup (Sun Conure).

As with most writers,Roma has a day job. She is a project manager in the IT field, working in various industries. She has a BS in Electronic Engineering, an MBA in Technology Management and a Masters in Project Management.

Her book, *Gray Shadows Under a Harvest Moon*, a collection of six trick-or-treat thrillers, is available at Amazon and most other book sellers. Her cat Nicky is, in fact, featured in one of the stories.

Follow her on Twitter at Roma Gray@romagraybooks13 or on her website http://trickortreatthrillers.com/.

Made in the USA
Lexington, KY
26 June 2019